SOUTHERN DECONSTRUCTION

SOUTHERN DECONSTRUCTION

Matthew H. Richardson

ISBN: 979-8-234-08414-9

PROLOGUE

NEAR THE HARNETT COUNY LINE, on the high west bank of the Cape Fear River, is a worn, one-room shack. The side of the shack facing the water has been painted red, white, and blue, but the colors form a Southern Cross. The paint says more than any book about The War.

Ten miles down, on that same bank, a rusted Fayetteville rifle hides under a foot of clay. It belonged to a boy with hope.

No one will ever find it.

INTRODUCTION

Christmas Eve, 1864
The Southern Coast of North Carolina

IMAGINE AN 18 YEAR OLD. He is five feet, ten inches, with sandy, autumn hair, and he's lying on his back in a canvas tent at a place called Sugarloaf, a spit of sand south of Wilmington on the eastern shore of the Cape Fear River. A northeast wind whips in from the Atlantic, and he shivers as the cold seeps through his blanket and his stiff grey coat. The brass buttons down the center of his chest, shiny a few weeks ago, have blued in the damp salt air. He rubs them nervously between the tips of his fingers and tries to close his eyes, but his mind flutters like the big grey gulls that whine in the wind above his head.

Sleep won't come tonight. Sixty-four warships carrying six-hundred cannons have come for a fight. They want Wilmington, the last seaport in the hands of the Confederate States of America. Without it, the South has no remaining supply line, and Lee's Army of Northern Virginia, once unstoppable, cannot make war.

Six-thousand Union troops sway in packed decks offshore, squeezing their rifles, waiting for the order, but before they storm the beach, they decide to play with fire. The USS

Louisiana, a 143-foot steamship, is packed with four hundred and thirty thousand pounds of gunpowder. A fuse system is rigged under its decks, ready to trigger the largest time bomb the Earth has ever seen. Its target: the impenetrable bunker of Fort Fisher, four miles south of the boy's tent.

Deep in the night, while Fisher is lost in dreams of Christmas' past, the Louisiana is steered into the breakers of the outer bar.

The anchor is dropped.

The fuse is lit.

At 1:40 a.m., the canvas of his tent vibrates like a bumblebee's wings. He doesn't notice until the posts begin to shake and the ground beneath him rumbles.

The thunder follows. It moves through him like a heavy ghost.

Like a kicked hive, his camp comes alive and hums with hysteria.

Orders are shouted.

A cannon is fired.

Men rush by the flap of his tent.

He sits upright and tries to gather himself, but his adrenaline has other plans. His nerves twitch in steady pulses, and his limbs tremble in cold fear. Against the shakes he rises, takes up his rifle, and steps out into the night.

"You're ready for this, Jim," he says to himself.

"You're ready."

February 18, 1865

Twenty Miles North of Charleston

IMAGINE ANOTHER, BUT A MAN THIS TIME. He is thirty-five, tall and thin, with a brushy moustache, fiery red hair and a temper to match. He is sharply dressed. At eighteen, his father cut off his allowance for spending too much on clothing. The lesson didn't take. His dapper style remains unmatched, despite the supply burdens of war. Today, he's sporting knee-high, polished jack boots from Russia. No one else is.

You might wonder who the man is trying to impress. He hasn't taken a wife. But The War is his mistress, and he chases her for glory. Until today, he never had to run. She came to him.

The man was one of the first to fire on Fort Sumter four years ago. The island of imported granite later became his post, and he defended his city from federal warships for over 500 days. As an artillery officer, he commanded the cannons and told others when to shoot them. His metal under fire was respected by his troops, but his ruthless discipline was feared by all. Cross him, and he'd hang you up by your thumbs.

It was good to work from home, a boat ride across the harbor and a short walk to the Charleston Club. Servants brought him fine food, and he'd debate the day's events with the elite men of his city. He paid for his club membership with revenues from his rice plantation on a tidal river thirty miles away. The man didn't have the physical attributes to toil in the wet, Lowcountry heat, so he bought dozens of people to do that for him.

Growing up, the man learned from those around him that he was different. He belonged to a small set of people that lived in bigger houses and had their own set of rules. These rules were codified in their words, actions, and customs. The code was enforced with power and blood.

The man learned the code from his father, and he eavesdropped as fancy men visited their three-story home and debated trials of honor in the parlor. "Honor," that thing that's hard to describe but everyone understands. He vowed as a young boy to keep his, and he dueled imaginary enemies in his backyard. *Ten paces...Turn... Steady...FIRE!!!* The practice would later serve him well as an adult.

Four years ago, the man stood in the crowd and watched the delegates walk down the aisle in ceremonial robes into the great hall in Charleston. His father was among them, and the last to sign the Ordinance of Secession. The man's heart was filled with pride when his father received the loudest ovation of all, fell to his knees, and gave thanks to God. Being educated in history, the man saw the coming war as an opportunity to cement his legacy and bring honor to his name. He enlisted quickly, and despite no military experience, he was appointed by the Governor to an immediate command.

The man believes that certain people, like himself, are superior to others in all things that matter. His life experience has confirmed this fact, and his identity is built around this premise. But today, he doesn't feel elite. His back is stiff from a slow ride in a rusted train car. The soldiers next to him aren't worth talking to, so he pulls a silk handkerchief from his pocket and polishes his boots. His battalion, along with all the others, is evacuating Charleston. At Cheraw, where the track ends, they'll give him his horse to ride. Then it's North, to fields of battle and One Last Stand.

His father named him Alfred.
Now he's Colonel Rhett.
He's still looking for a fight.

Slow down a wave:

A shiver as it hits your skin;

A shudder as it passes through you;

A pull as it takes you with it;

A push as it spits you out.

PART I

1

March 12, 1865

AS JIM MARCHED IN STEP along the rusted rails of the Wilmington-Weldon railroad, he carried a hidden weight. It had grown heavier in the night, and he was tired of internal debate. He fell out of formation into the ditch on the right and made his decision. Already lighter, he started jogging up the side of the line, his rifle at his side and his new haversack bouncing wildly against his hip.

Jim reached his captain at the front, caught his breath, gave his reasons, and asked for leave. His captain was receptive, and Jim was granted furlough, provided he could make it to Bentonville in three days. Jim thanked him twice, saluted and stepped off into the ditch.

The boys he knew waved goodbye as the column passed. Jim nodded back until it was clear, then he climbed the little hill and stood on the rail. Perched on the iron, one foot in front of the other, he watched as they disappeared down the track, pondering their fate, and already feeling left-out.

They were the Junior Reserves, the "seed corn" of the Confederacy, conscripted to fight in a war before they could call themselves men. Their first fight was on a beach, and they had seen the smoke pour out of the dunes as the big guns beat back the Union fleet. A few days later, the boys left their sandy camp and headed upriver.

Jim smiled at the cheering girls and saluted the old men as they passed through Wilmington. They were fresh Southern heroes, one-for-one in battle, but they had felt the power of the machines of war, and when Fort Fisher fell a few weeks later, their early glory seemed naive, and the boys stopped talking about it.

Jim had written Clara almost every day since he left for training in September. He wrote his letters alone, away from the nosy eyes of camp, and he took his time, placing care in every word. They had only been married a few months.

On his last day at the coast, he walked to a small live oak and fell under its shade in a spiral of doubt. A pencil was in his hand. A muzzle loading rifle lay across his lap. On the wooden stock was an empty piece of paper, waiting for his words, but Jim kept staring at the big block letters below the barrel:

FAYETTEVILLE

He loved that gun, forged at the Arsenal on the hill with machines stolen from Harpers Ferry. Jim had learned about it all in school, his teacher bragging that their local factory was churning out five hundred rifles in a single month.

Jim McClaren just needed one. It was sleek, sturdy, and never jammed. He kept it clean and shot it well, better than most of his class, each hit landing with a swell of hometown pride. But his pride had turned to terror with the news of Sherman's march.

He pushed away the doubt and started writing, and his right hand pled so hard that he broke the lead of his pencil. He sharpened it back with his pocket-knife and wrote on:

Clara, you've got to move!
Get out while there's time.
Go up North to your cousin's farm in Virginia.

When he finally finished the letter, he was sick to his stomach, and he couldn't bring himself to sign his name. He crumpled up the paper and threw it in the brush. She was a stubborn girl, strong and independent, and their little house was all they had.

Jim left the live oak and followed a game trail through the bushes and razor grass until he reached the edge of the river. The sun was almost set. He sat down, leaned back against his hands, and looked upstream, the horizon ablaze in deep orange over the back marsh and mirrored in the smooth sweep of a falling tide.

It was beautiful.
But so was she.
About ninety miles *that way.*

Dusk hit his neck with a cool shiver. He stood up from the hard, damp sand, brushed off his hands, and walked the quarter mile back to his camp. He eased into his tent, took off his shoes, and lay down under his blanket. He reached for his haversack and pulled out a copy of Harper's Weekly that he had bought off a boy from New Bern in the next tent over.

Jim stared at the cover of the magazine without flipping a page. What he saw shook his soul: Atlanta ablaze in black and white. At the bottom of the page, two bluecoats sat on a pile of busted Confederate cannons, watching the city burn.

In the dim light of the tent, the tricky flames started dancing, and when he finally closed his eyes, they were sunset orange.

In dream, the flames spread.
Atlanta...Savannah...Columbia.

Nothing had stopped Sherman.
Maybe nothing would.
And Fayetteville was next.

2

ACROSS THE CAPE FEAR RIVER FROM FAYETTEVILLE, weeks of rain had turned the Raleigh Road into a quagmire. Wagon wheels slid into slick ruts. Hooves sunk deep, and mules quit trying. Mud ate the shoes of the men that still had them, but they pushed on under the fierce eyes of their Colonel, who rode the lines on horseback and shouted at them to close the gaps.

There was little need to hurry. They had torched the covered bridge behind them, and the men knew it would take Sherman's engineers several days to build a replacement. They formed up tight until he rode away, then fell back again, lost in a daze of exhaustion. Their Colonel spurred his horse at the front, gaining distance from the ragged brigade he was beginning to hate. There was little glory to be had. All that was left was duty, and he was tired of holding the weight he had inherited.

When Colonel Alfred Rhett was only three years old, his father, Robert Barnwell Rhett, became a household name in South Carolina. In 1832, at an Independence Day celebration in Charleston, his father gave a speech against a Congressional tariff that would harm Southern trade. South Carolina should ignore the law, he cried to the crowd, and defend its rights with arms if it came to that:

> *"And if the madness of tyranny drunk with domination, here on the free soil of Carolina, the fire and the sword of war are to be brought to our dwellings, why, Sir, I say, let them come!...*
> ***The spirit of '76 is not dead in Carolina!"***

Four months after the speech, Robert Rhett became Attorney General for the State of South Carolina. Five years after that, when Alfred was only eight, his father was elected to Congress and went off to Washington, giving more fiery speeches and continuing to get his name in the paper. He represented the Colleton District of South Carolina, white men preserving a liberty that had brought them extravagant wealth and power, and he was a master at stoking their passions. He fought for state sovereignty, the expansion of slavery, and cheered secession decades before it was popular.

Alfred came of age under the cover of this great Southern shadow. The benefits were wealth and privilege. The burden was legacy, and it was heavy.

He would try to hold it anyway. His father had attended Harvard, graduating summa cum laude, and he sent three of his five sons to his alma mater. Alfred arrived in Boston Harbour in 1847 and crept down the gangway onto the Long Wharf with a trunk full of new clothes, the latest sporting magazines, a box of buckshot, and feathers for tying fishing flies. The west wind carried the first air of autumn off the maples, and it felt new and fresh and full of energy. He took a carriage across the city to Cambridge, eager to find like-minded friends and join a club, but he received no great welcome, and he saw in their faces that he didn't fit in.

By Alfred's junior year, the nation was in uproar over slavery, and there was talk of a great civil war. His father was labelled a "fire-eater" and a "traitor" in the Northern press. Alfred ignored the papers and tried to keep his head high as he crossed Harvard Yard each morning. There were other southern students in his class, but not many, and their fathers weren't in the news. Alfred felt like a foreign relic, and after his older brother graduated, he became more isolated and homesick. His father wrote a letter to the board complaining of the hostile conditions on campus, and they took a vote. Despite not finishing the curriculum, Alfred would return to South Carolina with a full degree. A few months later, his father resigned from the U.S. Senate after his life-long dream of secession failed. A few months after that, Alfred's mother died, leaving a gaping hole in the fabric of his family.

Back home, manhood was waiting. Alfred needed a way forward and a suitable career. He had sworn off law and politics, so his father gave him a small rice plantation and dozens of slaves. After a few years of keeping the books, he was unhappy and bored. The local society was ancient: the same families, the same fights, the same dinners, and the same dances. With his family's power steadily dwindling, Alfred searched for his own way up.

He would find it in the past, in an ancestor, Colonel William Rhett, a colonial war hero and a pirate hunter who captured the legendary Stede Bonnet in a great naval battle in the Cape Fear River. William was known for his hot temper, but he was cherished by the people of Charles Town after he saved the city from invasive attacks by the Spanish and French.

As Alfred stared at the hard grey tomb of Colonel William in the church yard every Sunday, he felt the same hot blood pumping through his veins. He'd always been a fighter, but he had no uniform and no command, so he looked for those that did. Now in his late 20's, Alfred began socializing with the Army officers stationed in the forts around the city. He loved the soldiers for their proud independence and prestige and stories of war in Mexico. The officers used him for his game-rich land and his famous pack of hunting hounds.

It was thrilling to ride the Lowcountry with the brass, chasing foxes like they did in England, but when the guns were cased and the bourbon bottles were empty, the common ground ended. These were professional soldiers, many of them West Point graduates, with careers and promotions ahead. Alfred was simply a planter, a second son with his life planned out, a life that looked like all the rest.

Years passed.
Life went on.

Rice was grown.
Dances were held.
Alfred kept hunting.

But the abolitionists did not go away, nor did the slaves in the fields, and soon there were ears again willing to hear the song of the fire-eaters.

Alfred's older brother, Robert Jr., picked up the family torch. He purchased The Charleston Mercury, and when he and his father put ink to paper, they didn't hold back. The family newspaper was loved and hated, but read by all, and their scathing editorials were reprinted throughout the South. Together, father and son fanned the flames, lashing out at northern tyranny and the degradation of the Founders' plan for America.

As their propaganda worked into the southern consciousness, the expansion of slavery in the West continued to divide the country, and secession sentiment reached fever pitch. Alfred's father ran for office again and won.

Robert Jr. was elected to the legislature by a landslide, and the Rhett family flame rose high once again. Alfred stood cooly on the sidelines, waiting for his moment, and polishing his guns.

3

AS THE LAST OF THE JUNIOR RESERVES disappeared down the line, Jim stepped off the iron rail and took the dirt road to the west. It was quiet in the cut pine lowlands, not a soul in sight, and Jim felt small against the distance ahead. He gave ten minutes of thought to turning around and catching back up to his company. Then he imagined Clara surrounded by a group of bluecoats, and he knew he wouldn't stop until he saw her again. There would be no more doubt.

It was fifty-five degrees, good for a long walk, and he kept a steady pace all morning. The road cut a straight line through a flat world of evergreen. Some of the older trees were stripped of their bark, but the only other sign of man was a rusty turpentine still that was too big to move.

He followed the road down a slight fall and entered a green swamp. As the path narrowed, his nerves caught the squeal of wood ducks that saw him before he could see them. He stood still and heard the quick flutter as they flew back and around, then circled high, waiting for the "all clear" to slide back in and finish their lunch.

An hour further and he entered an old world full of twisted live oaks and ancient cypress trees that lined the Black River. To his left, a big white house boasted four huge columns and towered above the sneaky water. The old mansion was quiet. No carts. No carriages. No smoke in the chimney. Jim followed the road down to the bridge, but an old iron gate blocked the way. He approached cautiously, expecting an ambush, but all he found was a wooden box nailed to the bridge post. The box had a small slit in its face. A hand painted sign was nailed above the box:

Beatty's Bridge – Toll Required

~~10 cents~~ 1 Dollar

Jim rolled his eyes at the cost of inflation. The little money he had was worth less every day. But he had the feeling he was being watched. He turned around and looked up into the windows of the big white house. Silence answered. He dug in his pocket and pulled out a Confederate dollar. With his back to the house, he held up his hand and waved the bill in the air, then folded it in half and shoved it quickly in the box. He slid his rifle under the gate stock-first, climbed over, retrieved his gun, and crossed the bridge without turning back.

Jim turned north after he cleared the swamp, then east at the next crossroads, the big house miles behind but still on his mind. He dug his fingers back into his pocket and pulled out what was left. He was down to two dollars, and he regretted wasting his money. No one would have known.

By early afternoon, it was quiet in the pines. Jim filled his canteen in a clear stream and gnawed through his last corn cake. He spit out the grease and filled his canteen again. The food gave him a little jolt, and he marched on steady for hours, until the road dropped out of the trees and fell a hundred feet before him. At the bottom of the hill, the road ended, and Jim saw the wide brown water of the Cape Fear River. He hurried down the slope, his legs finally free of the full force of gravity, and his heart pumping with the thought that he was half-way home.

4

The Mercury called for troops:

"The tea has been thrown overboard, the Revolution of 1860 has been initiated."

THE SECOND SON OF THE "FATHER OF SECESSION" answered loud and clear. Alfred dove head-first into the South Carolina army, and no one would stand in his way. In a few short years, he was promoted to Colonel and given command of Fort Sumter. There could be no better post. The fort was a symbol of all they fought for, their independence, their liberty, and it was *his* to protect. As he stood high above that hard island of rock and watched the steady swell of the Atlantic, for the first time in his life, he felt something all his own, and no shadow could reach him.

That was then.

Now he was standing in mud, resting his horse as the stragglers in his brigade crossed another swollen creek. Their half-hearted movement disgusted him, but he was tired of yelling. How had it come to this? He closed his eyes and tried to remember the light. It was only two years ago, but it felt like a dream. Another world. Something to read about in a book. But it did happen. He was sure of it. And what a heavenly light it was!

The abolitionist fleet had steamed into Charleston Harbor while he was eating lunch. He climbed up on Sumter's parapet, peered through the glass, and saw the stars and bars above nine Union ironclads. These were mighty new ships of war, word was they were completely unsinkable, and they were staging an attack.

Most men would have panicked. Alfred walked back down to the dining room and finished his lunch. His men stared at him, anxious and wild-eyed, but he made them wait. A gentleman doesn't hurry.

When he finished his meal, he ordered his men to put on their full-dress uniforms and take their posts. Then he climbed back up again and took in the view. The metal war machines were closer now, almost in range.

Alfred ordered the colors raised in every corner of the fort. Then he called the band to the top and told them to play "Dixie." As the tune echoed across the waves, he added a thirteen-gun salute in a demonstration of honor, symbolizing the original, sovereign colonies. The thirteen blasts marked the moment, a loud invitation to battle, and he knew that all of Charleston would hear it.

He turned his glass toward the city and saw a massive crowd already forming. On every rooftop and all along the waterfront, from the Battery to the tip of the Southern Wharf, he saw the black suits of the men, the wide white dresses of the ladies, the tan aprons of the house slaves, and the skitter of children.

Everyone was watching.

He turned back out to sea and steadied himself. The drill had been practiced a hundred times. His men were ready and accurate. He gave the order, and his brick castle came alive with thunder and smoke. The storm of fire was hot and fierce. His cannons struck the closest ship ninety times, sinking it to the bottom of the Atlantic. The rest fell back in retreat, and in one glorious day, Colonel Alfred Rhett had become a hero.

Now *his* name was in every paper.
People waved to *him* in the streets.

A poem was written by a great author about the battle:

To the bare embattled height,
Then our gallant colonel sprung--
"Bid them welcome to the fight,"
Were the accents of his tongue--
"Music! band, pour out--grand--
The free song of Dixie Land!
Let it tell them we are joyful that they come!
Bid them welcome, drum and flute,
Nor be your cannon mute,
Give them chivalrous salute--
To their doom!"

Four weeks ago, the music stopped. Charleston fell without a fight. Alfred's father packed up his printing press and fled the city. Alfred went North, still in his uniform. He was given a brigade of a thousand men. They had been running for weeks in a race to beat Sherman and join up with the rest of Johnson's army, hoping to make a stand somewhere in the Tar Heel state, but their numbers were dwindling at every roll call. Men ran off in the night, never to be seen again, and Alfred was desperate to keep his new brigade in the field.

As the shadows lengthened across the Raleigh Road, a thin soldier, coatless and shoeless, crawled out of the swollen creek and fell to the ground. The man lay curled on his side, shivering in shock and fatigue. Alfred drew his revolver and shot a hole in the ground, six inches from the man's head. The man got up quickly, face splattered in brown muck, fell back in, and kept marching. Alfred slid his pistol back in its holster, satisfied with his work. Then he climbed back on his horse and rode high to the front.

It's not easy being the son of a great man. Everyone expects to see something they like about your father in you. But you're not him. Deep down you know this, but you still try to carry something that slips through your fingers. You grow tired of grasping and find something that's yours alone. Once you've got it, and you feel it, you'll go through hell or North Carolina just to keep it.

5

JIM LOOKED OUT ACROSS THE COLD, MUDDY WATER of the Cape Fear and saw smoke rising from the chimney of the little wooden shack on the other side. He was glad to see it. Someone was home.

He walked down to the edge of the water and saw the ferry keeper chopping a pile of wood behind the shack. Jim waved and whistled, and the high pitch echoed across the water. The old, bearded man saw him, laid down his ax, and walked down to the landing. Jim watched as the old man untied the flat boat, shoved it free with a long wooden pole, then stood in the middle, working his oars in long steady sweeps.

Jim laid the barrel of his rifle against a thin cypress and reached into his pocket for the rest of his money. The old man slowed the flat boat as he neared the shore, and Jim made the jump. The old man said nothing and reversed his row.

Jim laid his rifle against the wooden rail of the boat and held out a dollar bill. The old man shook his head "no" and pointed to Jim's uniform. Jim realized the man was mute, so he nodded back in understanding and mouthed a "Thank you." The old man turned and looked upriver.

The flat boat bumped into the soft, western bank. The old man stepped off first. Jim followed and tried to thank the man again, but he was already walking back to his woodpile.

Jim's legs were stiff from the momentary rest, and he took small steps as he climbed a quarter mile up the trail until he reached the road at the top. The wooden sign ahead told him he still had 35 miles. He wouldn't make it before dark, but he turned North and kept walking.

Soon the trees fell away, and the country widened into weedy fields of faded cut corn and the plowed-under cotton of seasons long past. The old homes in the fields were quiet, and the road ahead was empty. A blanket of clouds matted the sky, and the air was silent and still. Nothing moved, not even a bird, and it seemed as if the land was frozen in time. Jim kept on, a solitary speck inching across the grey afternoon.

Sometime after midnight, he crossed the Cumberland County line. As he walked over Rockfish Creek, he leaned over the edge and looked down at the water below the bridge. It was high and deep, swirling cold and black in the dark. He crossed the creek and kept walking, his face forward, his steps faster now, trying not to look at the old wooden gate on the right. He'd spent too many tears trying to forget it.

Jim's father had quit farming after his mother died, and he sent Jim into town to live with his aunt. A month later, a neighbor found his father's body face-down on his kitchen table. Their little farm on Rockfish was auctioned off. Jim got the old packhorse and 500 dollars, put away by his aunt until he got married or turned twenty-one.

Jim was wishing he had that old horse with him now. He had never walked this far in his life, and he could barely move his legs, but he was almost home.

Almost.

The campfires were laid across the road and Jim could see the wooden barricade and the long shadows of a dozen soldiers against the trees. Jim froze, still far enough back to be out of sight, but sinking with the realization that he was too late. If he was going to see Clara tonight, he'd have to find another way.

Jim heard a roll of thunder from behind him that didn't stop. It was getting louder! He hurried off the road to the left and hid behind the trunk of a thick longleaf pine. He knew the sound, and he peered around the tree in terror. They were carrying torches, and Jim saw the flashes of the faces of the men of the blue calvary as they galloped toward his town.

He moved deeper into the woods, hands out in front of him, searching for a way around the roadblock, and tearing free of the vines and thorns that tugged at his clothes. A distant boom echoed through the forest. He moved faster, scraping and hacking through the brush until the ground under his feet gave away, and he found himself standing in a creek. He climbed back out, shoes soaked and cold, and he tried to take a breath. But he heard voices. At least he thought he did. He turned away from the sound and hurried, following the creek, searching for cover, until he came into heavy thicket, full of blackberry bushes and vines that hung in ropes from the hardwoods. He held up his forearms, lifted his knees in high steps, and forced his way through the thorns. Deep in the thicket, he crouched low and still.

He listened hard but only heard his own breath and the thump of his heart against his ribs. His head was pounding. Sweat was dripping down his chest. He unbuttoned his coat, and the numbness lifted and he felt a sharp cold pain in his hands. He held them up close to his eyes and flipped them over. They were scraped all to hell, but nothing was deep. He wiped the blood on his wet pants, unslung his haversack, and placed it on the ground beneath him. He slid down onto his back and used the sack as a pillow.

Above his head, a strange, orange glow reflected off the clouds, and thick smoke slid through the treetops, carrying the smell of destruction. Jim pulled his shirt up over his nose and his cap down over his eyes, worrying about her, and wondering if his hometown would be there in the morning.

6

"...the loss of Charles Town and its garrison would probably involve the most calamitous consequences to the whole state of South Carolina, and even perhaps beyond it."

George Washington, Council of War,
March 27, 1780

THE UNITED STATES NAVY DOESN'T TAKE KINDLY to defeat. Four short months after Alfred's victory, the Union landed thousands of men, took the marshes and sea islands surrounding Charleston harbor, and set up their guns. *Big guns.* On the first day of the barrage, they fired a thousand shots at Sumter. Four thousand more would follow over the next seven days.

The fighting was relentless, all day and all night, and the fort became its own kind of island hell. Bricks turned to dust. Flames licked the wooden beams. Eight men were blown to pieces. Forty-four were wounded.

Alfred stayed at his post, proud and defiant, but the blasts shook his body and dented his mind. One hundred and fifty tons of metal were hurled through the August heat, and Alfred began to feel like every ounce of it was aimed at his heart. He fought against the fear with rage, locked in his duty, and his men didn't cower. They shot back, with the few cannons they had left, but the big Yankee guns were too far away.

By the end of it, Alfred was numb. He no longer heard the blasts. He didn't smell the smoke that whipped around the walls and settled on the waves. In seven days, his castle had been reduced to a pile of rubble, and he cried when they left it for good. The people saw him weeping, but he didn't care. Something he loved was gone forever, and the place where it all started had become the beginning of the end.

Alfred didn't tell anyone about the nightmares. They were too strange and dark, and they eased up after a year. But they had come back in full on the road away from home. He was fighting off sleep, avoiding unconscious torment, waiting for sunrise still hours away, when he heard a familiar tune in a familiar voice, echoing through the rain outside of his tent.

That our sons, at their guns,
Have beat back the modern Huns,
Have maintained their household fanes,
and their fires!

"God Dammit. Burnett? What do you want?"

The flap opened and Alfred saw the smiling face of his younger brother.

"Just wanted a reprieve from this rain."

Burnett Rhett slid into the tent, sat down, and began pinching the rain from his brown, handlebar mustache.

"I can't sleep in this God-forsaken state, Alfred. You?"

"I almost was." Alfred sat up slowly. "You think Hardee will ever stop marching?"

"I bring you good news, brother. We halt just ahead and dig in. Looks like you'll get your first fight in the field after all."

Alfred sat up straighter. He was in the rearguard, and his brigade would christen the battle.

"Are you going to give me any of those guns?"

"I'll make sure of it! No Rhett's gonna face that many Yankees without some fire power."

Alfred didn't like asking his little brother for help. He'd done alright on his own thus far. Two other brothers had fought, but not for long. Edmund Rhett caught a lung disease early in the war and came back to Charleston. Robert Woodward Rhett, the youngest, was sent off to Germany for college, but rushed home at the start of the fighting. He was placed in the infantry and left for Virginia. He was killed at Cold Harbor, his first real battle.

Alfred's older brother, Robert Jr., inherited their father's intelligence and zest for power. As a member of the South Carolina legislature, he was excused from fighting, and he spent his days politicking in Columbia and writing for *The Mercury*.

With two brothers on the sidelines and one in the grave, the weight of the family had fallen on Alfred and the man sitting across from him. Andrew Burnett Rhett had stayed in South Carolina for college and gone to medical school. Then he went to work at a hospital in Paris, France to learn his new trade. Like Alfred, Burnett was placed in the artillery at the start of the war, but he got to leave home. He went to Virginia, joined Lee's army, and fought in the early battles. These were the glory days of the South, and Burnett was cited for gallantry. He took a break from the fighting in 1862 to marry a governor's daughter at her family's mountain home in Flat Rock. Her name was Henrietta Aiken, a blue-blood South Carolina princess. Alfred knew his younger brother was set for life, and on the outside, he was everything a Rhett should be.

Burnett had come home to Charleston after getting married, and he was put in charge of the city's artillery defenses. With a head full of honor and the confidence of a man who's already won, he kissed his new bride each morning and made his daily rounds on the waterfront, watching his older brother hold, then lose, the most important piece of property in the South.

Now Burnett was in command of the artillery that rolled with Hardee's army. He and Alfred had spoken little on the journey. It was their first time in the field together, and as they sat in the candlelight of Alfred's tent, they couldn't help but wonder which one of them was stronger, the better soldier, the better man.

Alfred was jealous of Burnett. It wasn't so much his brains or his success. It was the care-free way Burnett moved through life. He did it all so easy. The way he spoke, the way he stood. Even when he made a mistake it never seemed to hurt him.

Burnett was weary of Alfred. His older brother had no filter and no tact, but he never seemed to have any fear. Alfred always had to push it, consequence be damned, leaving the rest of the Rhetts to explain it to the world.

But they believed in blood, and they were far from home, and Alfred was glad to have his brother there. He looked him in the eye and told him so, which took Burnett by surprise.

"What's wrong, Alfred? Are you gettin' the jitters?"

"Hell no!" Alfred looked down. "I just wish I had more men to do it with."

"About that…" Burnett looked Alfred dead in the eye. "Your reputation has taken a hit on this campaign. I know we're in desperate times, but there are ways to keep discipline apart from brute force. If your men hate you, they won't fight for you."

"I don't see any other way." Alfred was defensive. "I never have."

"There's always another way."

"Oh? And what does The Great Doctor of Artillery recommend?"

"You remember what he told us." Burnett tapped his temple with his forefinger and smiled. "Tell them something they can't help but believe."

Alfred shook his head. "That's father's bullshit! There's been too much talk already. I'm sick of it. Everyone forgets this is a God-damned war, and I'll stick to my guns until it's over."

Burnett sighed and drew a half smile at his older brother. "So be it."

7

THE SUN ROSE BRIGHT THE NEXT DAY, and the woods were quiet again. Jim sat up, rubbed his eyes, and slid on his damp, sticky shoes. He was empty and hungry but felt the clarity of a new day. He dug through his haversack and pulled out his last piece of salt pork. He stuck the meat between his teeth and rose stiff-legged and stretched. Then he crawled out of the thicket using the trail he had blazed the night before.

He stood on the bank of the little creek and chewed his breakfast. It was greasy and bitter and tough, and as he washed it down with a handful of creek water, he debated shooting the resident fox squirrel shredding pinecones on the branch above his head.

"They'll hear the shot. And then they'll see the smoke if I cook the damn thing."

A few yards ahead, a bend in the creek made a deep hole. As he walked the bank toward it, he saw two redbreasts dart under a log. Jim kept his eye on the little sunfish. They hovered in olive-orange suspension, gently twitching their fins, oblivious to war or anything like it.

"If I had a hook or two, I'd have an easy..."

TOOOOOOOO!!!

The blast of a steamboat whistle interrupted his sentence. The fox squirrel darted up an oak tree and dove into its nest. Three more blasts followed, long and drawn, echoing up the creek bed and rolling up the sandhills.

"Reinforcements for Sherman," Jim said to himself.

"Must be from Wilmington."

"They sure didn't waste any time."

Jim had the sudden urge to move. He hadn't come all this way to hide! He would blend in fine. Just a local boy like all the rest. No one would know he was a soldier.

The woods were thick but easier in the daylight, and by late morning, he saw the backs of the homes that lined the side streets on the edge of town. He buried his rifle, jacket, and haversack under a pile of pine straw and threw a few rotten branches on top to mark the spot.

He slipped out of the woods and hopped the short iron fence of the Stewart's back yard. The big house was deserted. Trash was piled in the yard, and all the windows were broken, but as he looked out into the street, he saw that most of the homes were still standing. Hope! He jogged out into the street when he saw it was clear and turned the corner.

As he reached his front steps, he slowed, feeling like an uninvited guest. Maybe he was? He'd only slept in their little house a few times. Using his left hand as a brush, he scraped his thick brown hair across his head. He tucked in his shirt and pulled up his belt. Then he turned the worn brass handle, but the door was locked.

Jim knocked. No one answered.

He banged on the door. Nothing.

He yelled her name. Silence.

A range of possibilities, all awful, ran in sequence. He convinced himself that she had made it out, but as he turned away, he regretted not sending his last letter.

As he turned to leave, he heard a soft call from the back of the house. He jumped off the porch, ran around the side, and hurdled his short picket fence in one motion. When he landed, he saw her standing there, and six months apart was reduced to a moment.

Clara had endured Sherman's visit under the floorboards of their little backyard barn. Their old pack horse was taken first. She had heard them coming, flat on her back, trying not to breathe. Dust fell through the slits and into her face, and she lay there shaking as two drunk men walked off with the most valuable thing they owned. But now *he* was there. Her husband. And he was running toward her!

They collided awkwardly, and they both laughed. He grabbed her waist and pulled her close. She was dirty and smelled like manure, but it mattered little.

"I love you so much, Clara! I'm so glad you're alive!"

But Clara's smile faded, and her brown brows sank with worry. She took Jim's right hand, put hers inside it, and closed it tight.

"What's wrong, Clara?"

She started walking toward their small back porch, pulling him along. Jim saw that the back door was open.

"Look," was all she said.

Jim let go of her hand and walked into his house.

The floors and walls were empty. They'd been cleaned out. Their furniture, the dishes, the painting, their savings. Nothing of value remained.

A new kind of rage entered Jim's heart. He lowered his head, and his eyes fell upon a torn picture of Clara's mother on the floor in the corner of their kitchen. He cussed under his breath. Then he turned and walked outside, grabbed his wife, and squeezed her tight. He felt her sobs against his chest. Jim held back his own tears.

She was the first to speak.

"Kill as many of them as you can, Jim."

The words stuck in his chest like a railroad spike, and he pulled back, away from her. When he got the courage to look into her eyes, he saw a woman looking back at him, still beautiful, but serious, and older than before. Lost in the depth of her emerald stare, he felt small, like she was the one who should do the killing. But she put her cheek against his chest, and he wrapped his arms around her waist, and they fell back into place, together.

They spent the rest of the morning on the bare floor upstairs where their bed used to be. Then they slept for hours, hiding from the world below. When they awoke in the late afternoon, he dressed and kissed her lips at the top of the stairs and again beside their front door. There, she held out her hand. He took it and stole a long look at her green eyes. Neither spoke. They didn't know what to say. He pulled her hand to his lips and kissed it. She smiled at him with all the courage she had left.

"If I get pregnant, what are we going to name him?"

"Him?"

"I just have a little feeling."

“I don’t doubt it.” Jim blushed a little. “Let me think on it.”

Clara watched her soldier leave. Quiet took his place. Upstairs, the room smelled of pine and him. She lay back down, wrapped herself in immediate memory, and wept.

8

JIM SCRAPED BACK THE PINE STRAW, took up his rifle and gear, and shook off the wet sand. Cross Creek had already risen a foot, its water was rolling with silt, and he knew the Cape Fear would rise with it. But the Yankees held the crossing, if it was still there, and he couldn't swim the big river holding a rifle. As the rain fell off the trees and pattered Jim's head, he drew a new map in his mind. The first rapid was miles north, at the fall-line where he fished for shad and rockfish as a boy. It would be a full day's march on foot. His legs burned just thinking about it, but it would get him ahead of the bluecoats and out of harm's way.

As he rolled up his grey coat, his mind turned to Clara, her face and her hips still clear in his mind. Then he remembered her cold, hard order. With his heart under her command, he took up his rifle and held it tight, hoping to make it through town under cover of darkness.

At the top of Haymount Hill, Jim stared in disbelief. Beneath him, dozens of pyres lined the streets and thousands of men crowded the sidewalks. The Market House was still standing in the square, but the Fayetteville Observer was smoldering. Its editors had cheered secession from the start. Not anymore. The haze billowed heavy in the humid air, and the full moon played hide-and-seek with the clouds, casting an eerie glow on the scene. He needed to move. Now.

Jim knew that the road north would be blocked, so he cut west and then up and around, through the woods that lined the town. Soon his feet hit the hard wooden planks of Ramsey Street, and he turned and looked back to the south. He saw a few campfires in the distance, but the rest of the road was clear. He unrolled his jacket and buttoned it back up. He slid on his belt, took his cap out of his haversack, and put it back on his head. A soldier again, he started marching.

After a few miles in the dark, he came upon the remains of fresh earthworks, dug by the locals for defense of the city. They'd been abandoned in a hurry and debris lined the pits and the road beside them. He laid down his gear and gun and squatted low, picking and pecking through the old campsite, looking for some kind of food. He found nothing to eat, but in the back by the trees he found two old canvas tents, tied into tight rolls.

"Must have fallen off the wagon." Jim unfurled one of the tents, marked C.S.A. in faded white letters. It was in decent shape. He pitched the tent and threw in his gear and climbed inside. It seeped a little in the corner, but otherwise it was dry. He took off his wet clothes and lay on his back and listened to the steady patter of rain on the canvas. In minutes, he fell into a deep sleep.

9

ACROSS THE RIVER, ALFRED RHETT sat under a tarp with the rest of the Confederate officers. A yellow sheet of paper was passed in a circle. When it reached Alfred, he took a long look at the plan of battle, hand-drawn by General Hardee.

Their goal was only to delay Sherman, not defeat him. His army was too great. A single wing had 25,000 men. Hardee had only 8,000, but with them, he would dig in deep and buy Johnson time to consolidate their remaining forces at Bentonville. Thousands of men were on their way, moving up from the deep south on railroads and carts and bare feet. Only with sufficient strength could they hope to break the big blue machine that had torn though their homeland.

Alfred felt the weight of the moment to come. His men would dig a long, deep trench into a farm field between the

Cape Fear River to the west and a swamp to the east, marked on the map in his lap as "Black River." It was a natural pinch-point. The Yankees couldn't flank, and they could only bring so many men to the front. When they did come up, tight and exposed, Alfred would be there to face them.

Three big guns would be placed along his line: two in the middle and one on the right flank. The guns would help, but Alfred knew that success would depend on the hearts of the men in his brigade. Those that remained were tough and seasoned, but most of them were artillerists. How would they handle a Yankee charge in an open field? Would they hold and fight and bring him honor, or flee and leave disgrace? He thought of the headlines in the paper. The good and the bad. But the die had been cast long ago. If this really was the end, he'd go down carrying all that mattered, and all that made life worth living.

Hardee dismissed them, and the officers shuffled out into the rain toward their tents. It would be another sleepless night for Alfred, but a fight was looming, and he would have them ready.

10

March 14, 1865

JIM WOKE WITH THE SUN HIGH IN THE SKY and chastised himself for sleeping late. He scoured the old camp again, hoping to find something edible in the daylight. Finding nothing, he knew he'd have to do it himself, so he put a fresh cap in his rifle and muzzled a round.

He hiked a half mile down the drop, eyes tight, scanning the woods around him. He jumped a few rabbits, but they were gone in the brush before he could get a shot. He kept moving and found a thin game trail with fresh prints, inches deep in the mud. He followed the trail until he came to a bright clearing in the canopy formed by a newly-downed poplar. Jim jumped up on the long, straight trunk and walked gingerly to the roots, now upturned in a semi-circle disc of wet earth. Jim peered over the edge of the dirt, scouting the lowlands below. It made a good blind from any animal coming up the trail from the river.

"This will work," he whispered to himself. Then he waited, quiet and still.

***

Alfred was loading his pistol. A deserter had been caught leaving camp in the night. The man's hands and feet were bound with rope. Two soldiers pushed him to his knees. There he wept, begging for mercy, until he was gagged with a strip of red rag. Alfred ordered the entire brigade into a line to witness what was to come. He didn't bother giving a speech. They all knew why.

***

The young whitetail buck came up the trail in a hurry. Jim raised his rifle and braced it on top of the dirt. The barrel sank a half inch and rested. Steady. Jim squinted down the barrel, waiting for the deer to turn. It came to twenty yards, smelled Jim and froze.

Jim clicked his cheek with a burst of air. The buck looked right, then turned left, broadside. Jim clicked back the hammer, took two deep breaths, and heard the quick, light, "pow" of a gun from across the river. The deer heard it too and turned its head toward the sound, its white tail up and its long ears perking straight between its spiked horns, but it didn't run. Jim exhaled in relief, pulled the trigger, and the young buck fell.

***

Alfred ordered five men to dig a grave for the deserter. The rest of his brigade worked in the trench all day, hurling dirt over their shoulders to the southern side, and forming an earthen wall of cover that grew with each flip of the shovel. Soon only the tips of their heads were visible, and the pile of earth was six feet high. When Alfred was satisfied, he ordered his men to rest. They would need all their strength in the morning.

When their Colonel retired for the evening, half of the men fell asleep in the trench. The other half took to the trees by the river, hunting the woods for any kind of food.

11

FULL OF VENISON AND HEAVY, JIM STUMBLED DOWN the game trail in the fading light until he reached the high bank of the Cape Fear. At water's edge, he turned north. The bottomland was high and clear, full of hardwood that blocked out the undergrowth and made for easy walking, but his movement was slowed at the deep ravines where little streams that fed the river deconstructed the layers of time. He had to circle around these cuts, uphill where they weren't so deep, losing time and most of his patience along the way.

He reached the Little River, more a creek than its name suggested, but a challenge in the dark. He slipped down the muddy slide to the sandy bank, bent down, and filled his canteen.

He drank most of the bottle. It tasted like clay. Then he searched for a spot to cross. Finding none, he waded the stream, holding his rifle in his right hand and his haversack in his left, both high above his head. The water came up to his chest, and he eased himself across in soft half-steps. Then he climbed out, dumped the water out of his shoes, wrung out his pants, redressed, trudged up the slick slope, and walked on into the night.

The hardwoods along the river shone like Greek columns in the moon's reflection, and it became a new world. Jim felt the restless energy of a night alone, and his body fell in with the rhythm. The only sounds were the damp taps of his flat shoes against the ground and the hoot of a barred owl that hunted the lowlands.

He walked for miles, steady and sharp, until a thick cloud of fog settled down at midnight. Jim could hardly see five feet in front of him, and he was forced to use the river's edge as a bearing. The Cape Fear was almost to a flood, but there were sharp branches and trees sticking out from the cliff beneath him and jagged piles of driftwood lodged against the bank. His inside foot slipped twice, and he began to worry that he might fall to his death. Adrenaline sharpened his nerve, and he thought he heard a voice. He crept on slowly until he heard it again, then he stopped and looked across the river.

Through the grey mist, Jim saw the faint yellow halo of a campfire on the far bank. He crouched down and waited, hoping for a better look. He heard a man's voice, clearer this time, and the sweet scent of cooked fish caught his nose. Jim waited, unsure what to do, until the wind picked up, the fog lifted off the water, and he saw it all clearly.

Four men were gathered on a mud bank above a creek mouth. A man in a grey coat was holding a flat fish on a stick out over the flames. Jim felt a burst of relief, but it didn't last.

"They shoot deserters," he whispered to himself.

"But I have to cross, or I'll never get back."

He took two deep breaths and waited. Then he decided to break the ice.

"Who goes there?"

The men across the river looked up quickly.

"Who goes *there*?" a sarcastic voice called back.

"James McClaren, Junior Reserves!"

No answer. Jim waited.

"Cross! Now!"

Jim hesitated. "I can't swim with my rifle."

"Would you rather be shot by ours? Leave it!"

Jim squinted into the light. Four of the men had shouldered rifles, all pointing at him, and he instantly regretted breaking cover. Out of options, he laid his Fayetteville Rifle against the tree beside him. It hurt to let it go. Maybe one day he'd come back for it? Jim was staring at his gun when the bark above the barrel exploded with a heavy smack, and the crack of a shot echoed down the river. Jim fell backwards onto his butt, wide eyed and terrified.

"Cross!! Or the next one's in your chest!"

"Yessir! Coming!" Jim barked back.

He stood up fast and wrapped his left arm over the strap of his haversack so that the strap lay straight across his chest and the sack was on his back. He figured it would float. He scanned the bank and saw a slide of clay, not quite a straight drop, formed by a tree that had washed downstream. Jim approached the opening, sat down feet-front, and let himself go. He dug the wooden heels of his shoes into the slick clay as he fell, but the drop was too steep to matter. After twenty feet he landed, and when he opened his eyes, he was standing in water up to his thighs. The men were laughing.

"Good form! Now get your ass over here!"

Jim took another deep breath, readied himself, and lunged forward. The frigid river hit his chest and shocked the warm air out of his lungs. His arms were fast and wild as he tried to keep his eyes above the surface. In seconds, his legs were too stiff to kick and his hands were numb. He felt only the hot blood in the veins in his arms as he pulled them back in half-strokes. His haversack took on water, so he pulled the strap over his head. It rose to the top and floated downstream. He looked for the fire, saw he was only half-way, and began to panic, wondering with each wild slap if he had the strength to make it. He held his breath and resigned to a black death in the river, but his feet caught squishy mud, and he stood up and opened his eyes.

A dirty hand greeted him. Jim reached for it and was yanked up quickly. He stood dripping on shore, arms wrapped around himself, shivering fast like a wet dog. Three men had surrounded him. They were dressed in ragged pants of different colors. Only two wore coats, and one was missing a sleeve. He could already smell them. A tattered fishing net, a pile of shad carcasses, and an empty glass bottle littered the sand near their feet.

"You a deserter?"

"N....." Jim took a deep breath. "N..n..no, Sir."

"What are you doin' all the way out here then?"

"I was...on leave...to my home. I'm trying to get north...to my company."

Jim had honest blue eyes that looked too serious when he told the truth and too soft when he lied. In this case, they served him well. The man closest to Jim tugged on the sleeve of his new coat, turned and looked at the other men, and smiled with sly approval.

"Alright then seed corn. You made it just in time for supper!" The soldier stuck his arm in the ribs of the man next to him. "Give the boy a fish. He's even skinnier than you, Mac!" The rest of them laughed.

"Aww Bullshit!" The thin man waved off the others and handed Jim a stick impaling a thick white shad, its silver belly browned from the smoke of the fire. The man sat down on a log that a flood had left on the bank, holding a fish of his own. He motioned to Jim, and Jim sat down beside him.

The skinny man pulled the fish from the end of the stick, peeled back the skin, and pinched off a swallow of meat. "He's always talking. After all a times I's saved his ass, you'd think he'd be grateful."

Jim noticed the slur and smelled the man's breath. He nodded back quickly with a half-smile and turned his attention to the fish, but the other three men had inched in closer and stood in front of him.

"Look at you…fresh batch of seed corn!"

Jim thought about escape, but they were on top of him now.

"He's lucky he ran into *us.* Colonel Rhett woulda shot him where he stands. Just like all the other cowards. Tell him, Simmons!"

The one-sleeved man on the left took a step closer.

"Listen here, boy. Our Colonel don't mind killing. Been doin' it since the beginnin'. He was second in command at Sumter. A Calhoun was first. You know who John Calhoun is, don't you?"

Jim swallowed hard. "Yessir."

"See, this Calhoun was the President's nephew. The two of them get to jawin' about who makes better officers…West

Point men like Calhoun…or hard men like Colonel Rhett."

Simmons raised his left eyebrow and looked sideways at Jim.

"You ever seen a duel, son?"

"Nossir."

"Let me educate you then. They meet at a gentleman's club outside of Charles Town. Each man gets a second, and they follow the old code."

Simmons held up his hand. His thumb and index finger formed the shape of a pistol.

"Ten paces, and the word is given."

Simmons lowered his pistol barrel and pointed it at Jim's forehead. Then he paused for effect.

"FIRE!!!"

Jim flinched and tried not to show it. The other two laughed hard, but Simmons wasn't done.

"Now who do *you* think won?"

"Colonel Rhett?"

"You damn right he did! Calhoun fell deader'n a rock in that river behind you!"

Jim looked back at the water. When he turned back Simmons was in his face.

"And here's the kicker seed corn…" Jim felt the sharp poke of a finger on his breastbone, and the man's hot breath burned his nose. "General Beauregard is a man of the old code. He gave our Colonel command of Sumter."

Jim couldn't believe it. "You mean he took the place of the man he shot?"

"Of course he did! Damn, seed corn, you don't know *shit.* That's what honor required!"

Jim saw the others nodding in agreement, but their heads turned with the sound of a new voice coming down the bank.

"Simmons? Who in the hell is this? And why are you fillin' his head with horse shit?"

The new man came down the bank wearing a wide-brimmed calvary cap with yellow trim, a long grey coat, and leather boots that rose above his knees. When the man neared the fire, Jim saw a full black beard, deep blue eyes, and straight white teeth clenching the nub of a cigar. The skinny man beside Jim got up from the log and stood straight. Jim stayed seated, unsure of what to do.

"Where are you from son?" The cavalry man was looking at Jim.

"Near Fayetteville, sir. About twenty miles downriver."

The cavalryman turned to the others. "You see gentlemen…the boy just lost his town, a town his own government didn't even defend. I don't think honor is the appropriate lesson for tonight." Then he turned to Jim. "Boy, don't ever neglect the difference between honor and arrogance. That error has done more damage to this cause…"

Simmons took a step forward, rising to the challenge. "That's bullshit, Moore! And you know it!"

Moore looked down, drew a forced half-smile in the corner of his mouth, shook his head, and chuckled. Then he turned back to Jim.

"Well boy… you've lasted a whole night amongst these bastards. I think you've got the wits to figure honor out on your own." Then he turned back to the men, regaining command.

"We advance past the pickets at sunrise. I have orders to find a scout for our right flank."

The men were silent.

"Any volunteers?"

Simmons pointed a greasy finger at Jim.

"Seed corn knows the country."

Jim felt his stomach drop. Moore looked him in the eye.

"Well son?"

"I'll go where I'm ordered." Jim meant it.

Moore was impressed. "Good...You see that? The boy has more heart than all of you."

"I'd be happy to test that!" Simmons was still hot.

"No you won't!" Moore was tired of games. "To your guns. It's almost sun-up."

The men started moving. Jim stayed on the log, waiting for what came next. As the other soldiers stumbled up the muddy bank, Moore stayed behind.

"Where are you supposed to be, son?"

"With the Junior Reserves. In Bentonville."

"I'm Thomas Moore, Hampton's Cavalry." Jim shook the long, out-stretched hand and was yanked up off the driftwood bench.

"Brush that mud off your shoulders. And follow me."

12

March 15, 1865
First Day of the Battle of Averasboro

JIM FOLLOWED MOORE UP THE SLICK CLAY BANK into the trees. They came upon the edge of the field where a camp was coming alive in the foggy twilight. Half of the men were still asleep on the ground, some on blankets, others propped against the pines. Less than half wore shoes. Jim wondered if they could even fight.

As they moved into the soggy field, Moore pointed south to the wood line, hued black against the grey dawn. "Rhett's line is too thin to extend to the river. We can't cover his flank. You'll ride with us to the trees, dismount, then veer into that corner." Moore was getting serious now. "Move past our pickets. Wait there in the woods. If you see any more than a dozen Yankees coming your way, you high tail it out of there, run back here, and tell the first officer you can find."

"Yessir!" Jim was ready.

Moore picked up his pace, and Jim stumbled along behind until they reached the edge of the camp. Four saddled horses stood apart, tied to a metal stake in the ground. Steam rose from their sides and blended with the fog. Behind these, a dozen troopers were already mounted. Clouds of breath shot from the muzzles of their anxious rides. The troopers tipped their caps as Moore approached. Moore tipped back, and Jim heard the rattle and the chink of harness as they spun into a line.

Moore walked to the stake and ran his hand along the neck of a riderless mare, sleek and brown and white. He reached under and around and tightened the saddle. Then he looked back at Jim.

"You know how to ride?"

"Yessir. Owned three horses on the farm."

"Were any of them fast?"

"One was."

"Was that one yours?"

"Yessir," Jim was hiding a grin.

"Saddle up!"

Jim reached over the saddle, slid a slick shoe in the stirrup until it caught, and threw his right leg over. Moore climbed fluidly onto a speckled stallion and pulled a double barrel shotgun from the side of the saddle. Jim watched in awe as Moore flipped open the breech with one hand and began to check the shells.

An older soldier carrying a steaming tin cup walked up to them and smiled. "Where the hell are y'all going at this hour, Moore? They've got us digging these ditches all morning."

"I aim to ascertain the strength of our enemy." Moore snapped the breech closed and looked down with a half-grin. "Regardless, I'll be back before you're done with breakfast."

The old man shook his head, amused. "Godspeed! If you run into General Johnson, tell him to quit backing up! We'll all be Virginians by summer at this rate!"

"There's worse places to be than Virginia, though not many." Moore grinned in full.

"I suppose you're right. 'Least until Uncle Billy gets there!"

"You said it!" Moore tipped his cap, spun his horse, and addressed the line of troopers.

"They should be less than two miles south, moving up at us. Use the creek beds for cover. Slow their advance. Engage, but don't over-expose. And gentlemen, they all have Spencers now. If you get in a firefight, you had best aim true!"

The troopers grunted with unanimous approval. Moore kicked his horse. The rest did the same. And they were on the move.

Jim waited until he had enough room, then kicked his horse to a trot. The hoofbeats were soft in the wet sandy soil. He matched their speed quickly as he rode into the grey, half eager and half afraid of what lay ahead in the trees.

***

A quarter-mile away, in front of the trench, Alfred ate his breakfast on his feet in stiff anticipation. He imagined his brigade as an anvil, his guns the hand of justice. As he chewed a thick piece of bacon fat, he closed his eyes and saw his name on the cover of *The New York Times*:

RHETT'S REVENGE IN CAROLINA!

"Pardon me, Colonel." The Captain from Company C approached carefully, interrupting the dream. Another deserter had been caught in the night, and the men needed orders.

"You know what to do."

Alfred swallowed hard.

"Line them up."

13

AS THE CLUSTER OF TROOPERS reached the woodline, Moore held up his fist, and the men fanned out in a straight line. Jim held his horse behind the formation, six to the left, six to the right, and Moore in the center of the road.

Moore pointed a black, gloved hand at Jim, motioned downward, then pointed to the corner of the field.

Jim nodded, hopped off, and handed the reigns to the next rider. The trooper handed Jim a rusted pistol in return. The gun felt heavy and awkward in his hand.

"You might need this. Only six shots. Don't waste any of them."

Jim nodded back.

Moore pushed his fist forward, and his men advanced.

Jim hung back in the field, trying not to lose sight of the

men in the mist. When they were gone, he started walking along the edge of the field, and the grey blanket of clouds above his head opened in a steady drizzle. It pooled on the branches of the pines that lined the field and fell in dollops on his forehead. He wiped his brow and avoided the low spots as best he could, but his shoes were soon caked and heavy with mud.

In the woods to his left, Jim saw a small ravine that fell towards the river. He'd have to cross it somehow, and as he moved down the tree line, he focused on finding a way. The ravine narrowed near the far back corner of the field. The little canyon was fifteen feet deep, but only about five feet wide. Jim picked up a stick and scraped the mud off his shoes, then threw the stick on the ground. He got a running start, squeezed the pistol tight, leaped hard off his left foot, stretched out, and made it over clean.

Now, he was in the woods. As the trees closed in around him, Jim grew tense, and his eyes scanned left and right, expecting a shot at any time. He crept forward, and soon he saw the grey backs of the men of a picket line.

They saw him too. An older, bearded man left the line and walked towards him. The man took off his worn grey cap and wiped his thin hair back with his hand.

"You a scout, son?" The old man was whispering.

"Yessir." Jim whispered back.

"They're at the next creek by the church, building a bridge." The man pointed for effect. "Just up the road there."

Jim nodded in silence. Then he crept down toward the river, away from the flank of the picket line, until he reached a small creek bed. He stood at the edge, and leaned against a pine, eyes wide, scanning hard for any trace of blue.

***

Out in the field, the South Carolina infantry was ordered up out of the trench and into a line. The coward was brought forward. Alfred stepped up to meet him.

"You are guilty of the crime of desertion. By the power given to me by the State of South Carolina, I hereby sentence you to die." Alfred cocked his pistol.

"May God have mercy on your soul."

***

Jim heard a faint shot from his rear. As if in answer, the woods in front came alive with rifle fire. He heard ten shots in half as many seconds. More followed. These were closer. Then it was constant.

***

Alfred was wiping down his pistol when he heard the rattle of fire in the woods to his front. He squinted through the mist, expecting to see blue calvary emerge onto the field in front of him. None came. He looked down the line at his men. They had all moved back into the trench, without orders. Alfred mounted his horse, already agitated and restless.

A rider came with orders from General Hardee for Alfred's remaining skirmishers to advance. Alfred spurred his horse and rode across the field to the rest of them, fifty or so, fanned out at the tree line, all staring into woods. They didn't turn around as he approached, so Alfred announced his presence.

"Forward!"

They moved, but the men weren't in a hurry. Alfred yelled louder.

"Now!"

They were parallel with Jim a minute later. The men on the right flank saw him first. Jim stood still, squeezing the pistol, half-embarrassed that he wasn't with them with a rifle in his hand. They passed by him, slow as ghosts. Then they were gone, and a new kind of melancholy took their place.

These men had nothing left. Why were they attacking? What was there to gain? Territory? They'd already lost what mattered. It sure wasn't money. They had none. His father had told him it was about freedom. A peoples' right to govern themselves. But his father had died, never fighting like the others. Jim didn't want a war. He wanted a family. He wanted a chance. But the Governor of North Carolina had told him he had to.

He heard the skirmish line make contact. It fired in unison and the crack echoed through the trees. A cannon blast shook the ground. The line fired again a minute later. A scream in the woods raised the hair on his neck. Then more shots, but these were close! Then he saw them, the same men, moving back, this time in retreat. He watched as they dipped behind the pines, took a shot, ran back ten yards, crouched behind another tree, reloaded, pointed their long rifles, and fired again.

***

Alfred sat in the field on nervous edge as the sound of the battle drew closer. A dozen grey jackets emerged slowly from the woods. His picketers were back where they had started. He turned to his aide and sent a message to his main line. In seconds, three companies left the earthworks, fanned out in the open field and began marching toward him.

They moved on the double across the field in a perfect line, flags high and bayonets fixed, and what a beautiful sight it was. As they passed, their colonel pointed to the trees.

"They took your homes. Now take their lives! Men of Carolina, give them back some Hell!"

***

A new sound came through the trees that Jim had never heard before, but he knew exactly what it was, clear and sharp through the fog of battle. A pop. Three seconds. Another pop. Three seconds. Pop!

"Spencers!" Jim whispered to himself. The blue calvary was closing in. Jim left his tree and moved toward the river. In a hundred yards, he reached another ravine, a little deeper than the first. He slid down feet first to the bottom and leaned back against the wall. He covered his chest and then his face with wet leaves and pine straw and stared over the ridge ahead.

In a minute, he heard hoofbeats. He squinted through the shield of leaves as four riders approached. Jim couldn't tell whose side they were on, and he didn't want to find out. Slowly, without making a rustle, he drew the revolver up to his belly. He squeezed the splintered handle in both hands and pointed the barrel at the ribs of the rider who was crossing the ravine twenty yards upstream. Jim didn't shoot. They hadn't seen him, and they kept on. He lowered the gun and started breathing again.

14

AFTER A TENSE MORNING, ALFRED took a long breath. He had been informed that his skirmishers had retaken the lost ground. Free of the weight of prospective failure, he had an urge to talk to someone about the day. It should be someone important, like the Generals perched on horseback a half mile back, watching his performance. As Alfred trotted back in their direction, he rode high. This was going well. His aide followed in a hurry, trying his best to keep up.

Theodore Northrup, chief of scouts for General Kilpatrick's Union cavalry, rode steady through woods with three of his best men. Northrup was only twenty-one, but he was confident and seasoned. He had been fighting the rebels for four years, and he carried a lead bullet in his right shoulder from a battle outside of Washington, D.C. Northrup's loyalty to his commander earned him a new title, and he was making the most of it.

Northrup and his men were not wearing uniforms when they stepped into the open field at Averasboro. That would be stupid. A scout's job is to blend in, to get behind enemy lines. Fake a southern accent, get into their camps and their homes, find out where they are and where they're going. Don't forget to lie and cheat, and always steal anything of value.

Ten days prior, Northrup's men had plowed through Wadesboro on their way to Fayetteville. They took everything they could find from anyone they encountered. Even the Episcopal Bishop of North Carolina, Thomas Atkinson, became a target. Northrup's men entered his home, put a gun to his head, and took his watch, his clothes, his food and his horse. After all, this was war, and Northrup was good at it. The people of the South had quickly learned to hate him.

This morning, Northrup was tasked with obtaining the location of Hardee's army. Skirting the skirmish on their right, he and his three scouts had cut through the woods close to the river and emerged a few hundred yards from Rhett's main line. In the mist and fog, they looked like any other soldiers.

Alfred saw them first. Four riders in a cluster. They had to be important. Was it Hardee? Taliaferro? Eager to discuss the morning's success, he turned his horse toward them.

The scouts saw the yellow trimming on the coming rider's uniform and knew it was someone important. Northrup pulled his pistol, felt the nagging pinch of the old bullet in his right shoulder, and slid the gun under his coat. The click of the hammer made his horse twitch.

"Easy boys. Let's see who he is first."

Alfred rode up to meet them. "Where are Generals Hampton and Taliaferro?"

"They are right back here a short distance on the road." Northrup tried to hide a smile.

Alfred was silent.

Northrup broke the bad news: "You will have to come with us."

Alfred was baffled, and his face flushed in anger.

"You ridiculous ass! Do you know who you are talking to?"

Guns drawn in a flash! The closest scout stuck the cold tip of his Spencer in Alfred's ear. The others backed him up, and Alfred was instantly surrounded.

"I'll have you all shot for this." Alfred was furious, but the reality of the situation hit him fast. Outnumbered and tricked, he was now a prisoner, his liberty taken for the first time in his life. Worse, he had failed in his first battle in the field. He cursed under his breath as the third scout grabbed the reigns of his horse.

"Settle down. We'll take good care of you." The man was smiling. Alfred turned red with rage. The scouts kept their guns on their prize, and together, they headed for the trees.

15

JIM WAS STILL LOOKING TO THE SOUTH, and he didn't hear the hoofbeats until the riders were crossing the creek beside him. He recognized them quickly, the same four men, but this time, their pistols were drawn on a tall, thin Confederate officer on a big brown horse, wearing the nicest uniform Jim had ever seen.

"They've got a General," he whispered to himself. Jim pulled up the revolver and opened the cylinder. "No!" It was half empty, holding three bullets, all swollen with rust.

Jim had never shot at anyone before, but he wasn't a coward. He'd get off his three shots and make a run for it, back toward his lines, and tell an officer what he had seen. He raised his hands through the leaves, left hand wrapped on top of his right, squeezing the wooden handle. He let the first rider cross. Then he closed his left eye and aimed the barrel at the second rider's ribcage. He steadied his breath.

Exhale. Inhale. Exhale. Steady.

Jim squeezed the trigger.

A wet, soft, *click* answered his pull.

Misfire. Jim's arms fell limp at his sides, and he pinned his back against the berm, staying as still as he could, hoping they hadn't seen him. He squinted through half-slits as the rest of the riders crossed the creek, guns still drawn on the fancy man in the middle. The Yankees rode high and proud, and a wave of anger rose up Jim's neck and into his forehead.

"Why didn't they give me a rifle? Instead, I get this ol' rusty pistol with three spoiled rounds. I could have taken down a few and saved whoever that was."

But his spirit faded with the riders in the trees. He wanted to slide into the creek at his feet and let it carry him down into the river. He'd be home by dinnertime. She would be sitting there, and the little things would matter. But it wasn't his call. *This* was what mattered. So Jim McClaren rallied his mind with the reserves he had built over eighteen years, and he stayed upright, at post, on the right-flank of a desperate army of a crippled new nation in the woods upriver from his hometown.

He was captured thirty minutes later.

The blue wave came like they do at Fort Fisher.

All he could do was put up his hands.

PART II

16

ALFRED'S THIN BLUE EYES twitched left and right, waiting for the opportunity to spur his horse and flee, but the scouts were seasoned riders. Their guns stayed on him, even in the thick spots, and in minutes they emerged from the woods into the open clearing of Raleigh Road. An endless snake of men, wagons, horses, and caissons filled the space. The whole mess of it was slithering toward his brigade a few miles back, but Alfred had missed his chance at glory, and he hated them for it.

He felt their stares as he passed them. Some cheered. Some called him names. Others just laughed. He kept his eyes above them, afraid they'd see his shame, and determined to keep the honor he still had.

The blue riders reached their new headquarters, set up

hastily in a cooper's shop on the side of the road. The men dismounted and Northrup ordered Alfred to the ground. Eager to show off his new prize, Northrup headed straight for his boss. He found General Kilpatrick on the porch, leaning lazily in a rotten chair that looked like it could collapse at any second. He stayed seated as his lead scout approached.

"Hello, Northrup. What troops are these we are fighting?"

"Taliaferro's Division from Charleston. I have one of the brigade commanders with me."

Kilpatrick jumped up quickly. "The hell you have! Bring him to me!"

Northrup saluted and turned and went to retrieve the colonel. He hoped this gift would improve his boss's morale. It hadn't been a week since the ambush, and they had nearly lost it all.

A few days before they entered Fayetteville, four thousand rebels had crept through the scrub oaks of the Sandhills and hit them at night while they were sleeping.

Kilpatrick woke with the commotion and walked out onto the front porch of the farm house he had confiscated for the night. He rubbed his eyes twice, unable to believe what he was seeing. Men were slashing with sabers, spearing with bayonets, and blowing point-blank holes in one another with pistols. Dozens of bodies already lay in the yard.

Before he could think of what to do, two rebels rode up to the porch, but they failed to recognize him in his underwear.

"Where is Kilpatrick?" They demanded.

Kilpatrick raised his hand and pointed: "Over there! Kilpatrick went that way!"

The rebels took the bait and rode away. Kilpatrick jumped off the porch and hid in the trees. His men rallied and drove off the attackers, but the damage was done to his shaky reputation. The papers called it "Kilpatrick's Shirt-Tail Skedaddle." He didn't find it funny, and five days later, hiding from the rain on another front porch in Nowhere, North Carolina, he was eager to take it out on the southern aristocrat that now stood before him.

"Identify yourself, soldier."

"Colonel Alfred Rhett."

"How did they take you?"

"It was nothing but a damn Yankee trick!"

"Ha!" Kilpatrick looked up at Northrup, who was trying to hide a smile.

Alfred scowled at the little man in front of him. "Laugh if you wish. There's fifty thousand fresh men waiting to fight you in South Carolina!"

Kilpatrick's grin turned to a sneer. "And if that's the case we'll have to hunt every swamp down there to find the damn cowards."

Alfred stayed silent.

"Northrup." Kilpatrick kept his eyes on Alfred.

"Yessir?"

"Take him to General Sherman."

Alfred's neck hair stiffened. He was going to the top, and he would represent not only himself and his family, but the entire State of South Carolina. The weight felt different and heavy like a stone. He had seen it on his father's face, and it frightened him. As he followed Northrup up the steps, his hand reached for the pistol at his hip, but all it found was the damp leather of his holster.

This time there would be no guns.

No seconds.

No code.

He tried to remember who he was, but his heart wouldn't let him. He was someone else now, though they still called him "Colonel."

The door had no handle, so Alfred pushed it open. He walked in chin-up and straight, hoping to make an impression. General Sherman was leaning back in an armchair at a wooden table with three other officers, smoking a fresh cigar. The General's hair was wet and uncombed, and his jacket was unbuttoned, revealing a sweat-stained undershirt. He rose when he saw his new prisoner.

"Colonel Rhett. Hello! I hear you've made acquaintance with Captain Northrup, our chief of scouts."

Alfred nodded, ignoring the jest. Sherman pointed around the table.

"I believe you know some of us. Here we have General Slocum, General Davis, and this is Major Hitchcock."

Alfred walked to each man and bowed and shook hands. Then he took a step back, closed his feet, and stood at attention.

Sherman was intrigued by his prisoner. Birthed in Southern flame. Offspring of secession. American traitor. Now homeless at the hand of his army. Still digging in.

For the past five months Sherman had ignored the critics of his Great March, North and South. To end the War, the South had to be beaten into submission, and its people must pay the cost for their treason. To some he was a terrorist. To others, a great surgeon, tearing the body apart so that it might be saved.

It wasn't saved yet, and they couldn't let up. His men were tired and longed for their homes, and he felt the sharp resolve of his inner circle soften with the spring. But the enemy hadn't quit. Not yet. He had torn through their land, but what about their hearts? Was anything left? Tonight, he'd put a scalpel to their prince and probe.

"At ease Colonel." Sherman tipped his cigar toward the only empty chair at the table. "You're among old friends, and you're just in time for supper."

17

JIM TRIED TO KEEP UP with the three blue soldiers in front of him. Another was behind him, telling him to hurry in an accent that felt foreign, but now that he was out of the battle, he had lost the fear of being shot. His eyes were dead ahead, his mind racing, wondering where they were taking him and what was supposed to happen next.

They emerged from the trees and stopped at the edge of the road. They stood there and waited as a hundred men in blue marched by in formation. After they passed, Jim felt the hard poke of a rifle barrel in his back. He turned around, and the blue soldier behind him pointed his finger at a group of rebel prisoners sitting in a cluster twenty yards ahead.

The prisoners were surrounded by a dozen armed guards. Jim walked up and sat down at the edge of the group and looked back at his captors. They saw him sit down. Then they slipped back into the woods.

The wind blew hard in the late afternoon, and the pines that lined the road see-sawed wildly above Jim's head. He sat as still as he could, watching the trees bend with the blows, each gust carrying the burnt smell of powder. A cannon was fired. Then another. The men turned their heads toward the sound. A short soldier in a blue cap stood over Jim and held up his rifle. "Don't any of you think of makin' a run, unless you want a date with Mr. Spencer." The soldier tapped the breech. "Got enough in here for all of you."

Jim scanned the group and counted twenty prisoners, himself included. They were all ages, a mix of men, ragged and soiled, eyes glazed and hollow, looking off to somewhere better. Jim looked to the south. He could be home in a few hours.

A company marched by them, four across and steady. They looked well fed, well dressed, and utterly serious. Twenty wagons followed, pulled by massive mules. Then three big cannons. Then another company, and another. It was a parade of power, and Jim wondered if it would ever stop.

As the light grew dim, they were called to their feet and ordered to march. They halted after two miles at a makeshift pen of small pine logs and crooked boards. They entered like sheep and joined fifty others. Jim looked for open space and sat down in the wet earth and leaned his back against the jagged rail. The firing died out with the day, but the clouds opened in a chilly trickle. Out of adrenaline, Jim wrapped his arms around himself, exhausted and trying not to shiver.

Jim saw a boy about his age walk toward him. He stood up to meet him, suspicious of a threat. The boy's grey coat looked new, unlike most of the rest. He stopped a few feet from Jim and held out his hand.

"I'm Benjamin Chester, from Cheraw. Just call me Ben. It's easier." The boy was talking quickly.

"How'd you get captured?"

Jim shook the thin, cold hand, but it squeezed back solid.

"Jim McClaren. Junior Reserves. From right down river. I was trying to get to Bentonville, but the cavalry used me as a scout." Jim pointed back down the road. "I got picked up in those woods."

"Me too."

Ben seemed unworried, even confident. It was strange to Jim. Was he enjoying himself? Jim sat back down, but Ben slid down beside him.

"They gonna give us anything to eat?"

"Hell yes!" Ben elbowed Jim's arm. "Better than our shit rations for sure." Ben reached into his pocket and held out a mashed johnny cake.

"This will keep you going. I'm holding out for that Yankee beef!"

"Thank you." Jim had already taken a bite of the hard disk of corn flour.

"Ain't nothin."

Jim could feel Ben watching him as he ate.

"Being captured ain't so bad you know. It's sure better than being shot at. How many battles you been in?"

"Two. Fort Fisher and here."

"You seen the ocean!?"

"We were camped there for a few months."

"What was it like? I always wanted to see it."

Jim looked up and tried to remember the Atlantic. He saw the white foam of the waves, the pelicans diving, and the big loggerhead that laid her eggs near their camp. A lonely cannon fired, breaking his salty dream.

"Man, it's cold in this rain…The ocean? It's awful mighty. Bigger than the pictures. It just goes on as far as you can see to the curve of the Earth. Sometimes it's calm and blue and clear. Sometimes it's windier than hell and all you can do is stay inside."

"Did you go swimmin'?" Ben was smiling now.

"Whenever I could."

"I swam the Pee Dee in the summer. Big catfish up and down that river."

"You ever get any rock?"

Ben nodded with his finger to his lip and twitched his eyes at the Yankee guard that was eying them from behind the rail. Jim understood and nodded back, and they sat in silence for the next hour, watching the rain fill the footprints that scattered the floor of their outdoor prison.

18

ALFRED TOOK A SEAT AT SHERMAN'S TABLE and placed his napkin in his lap and looked around. It was strange at first. Two of them, Slocum and Davis, had served in Charleston before the war, and Alfred knew them well, though that was years ago when war was only a theory they discussed in the clubs. Now it was life. It was him. He had the hardness of men who have stood at the wall and taken the bombs, and he wanted them to see it.

The wine was poured and the food laid down and the men began to chat freely. Sherman sat quietly and listened, observing the old camaraderie. He would put it to the test. If his hunch was right, it would only take a spark. This prince was reared in political arson.

"We caught up to you pretty quickly again, didn't we Colonel?"

Alfred finished chewing before answering.

"My men are from the coast, General. Artillerists. They know nothing of woodcraft."

Sherman chuckled. "Isn't it more about numbers at this juncture?"

"I'd say it's a question of leadership."

"Now that's a loaded word! I've noticed you Charlestonians have been quite critical in that regard. Your esteemed President…he isn't very popular nowadays, is he?"

Alfred took the bait and came out swinging. "Davis is a damn fool! If things had been properly managed your march through Georgia would have been a disaster."

Sherman glanced knowingly at his generals.

"A disaster? Enlighten us."

"You were fortunate that we allowed you to march on our country without a great battle. Sure, we would have lost thirty to forty thousand men, but we would have saved our cities."

Davis jumped into the fray. "But you can't afford to lose thirty thousand men, Colonel! You haven't got the men to spare now!"

"Oh yes." Alfred looked Davis in the eye. "We have plenty of men."

"They're not in the field."

"They're available. I will undertake in one month to raise one-hundred thousand men for our army with one cavalry regiment."

Sherman rolled his eyes. "And what will *they* be worth? How long can you keep such an army together? How much fighting will such men do?"

"Oh, just as good as any others." Alfred's chin was high.

"Just let me have my regiment to do it with, and I'll raise the men, and make 'em do good fighting too."

"You can't be serious."

"If I don't raise one-hundred thousand men in one month's time they may chop my head off."

"These men you speak of won't fight. Your army is shrinking by the day."

Alfred took a long sip of wine and felt the warmth of attention among equals of importance. He placed his fork beside his plate in perfect alignment. Then he raised his napkin and brushed the corner of his lip, folded it, and placed it back in his lap. He had been at this table before, many times, as a child and a man. Liberty is not reserved for the weak. He would hold his ground.

"Conscripts are just as good as any other soldiers. Discipline's the thing! All you have to do is establish the principle."

"Conscripts? They run away in droves. They come to us with their hands up, begging for food."

"Cowards. And most don't make it far. I've shot twelve men myself in the last six weeks and not long ago, I took a pack of dogs and went into the swamps and in three days I caught twenty-eight men with them."

Sherman put his hand on his chin and pondered a response. Was there any more to say? It was the same in Atlanta, Columbia, and all the towns along the way. *These* people. This arrogant class. And they never stop talking.

"Suppose I'm mistaken…this country cannot sustain itself without its institutions. The thousands that follow your army like a long, black train. They will pollute your cities and drain every bit of your wealth."

Davis jumped in again. "And what would you have us do

with them?"

"Simple. Those miserable miscreants should every one be killed."

Davis winced. Sherman didn't flinch. His stern brown eyes circled the table, and as he looked into the faces of his men, he knew the lesson had taken.

"That's a favorite hobby of mine." Sherman paused, letting the barb catch. "And there *is* a class of people in the South who must be exterminated before there can be peace in the land."

Everyone turned to Alfred, waiting for an explosion. But he took another long sip of wine and ate the second to last piece of beef on his plate. Then he placed down his fork and knife, wiped the corner of his mouth with his napkin, folded it, and smiled.

"I still can't believe I was gobbled up like that."

Sherman sensed the shift and let the prince off the hook.

"It happens in war. My scouts are brave men, and officers dressed like you make attractive targets."

Alfred held up his arms in mock surrender. "It was a dirty trick, I tell you! Soldiers in disguise. It's not a proper way to wage war."

Sherman took a long draw from the nub of his cigar. "You'll have to let it go. You weren't the first, and you won't be the last."

"No, General. I will give you that much. This war will go on, with or without disguises."

Sherman blew a long waft of smoke across the room, placed his right elbow on the table and looked down at the inch of rolled Cuban between his thumb and forefingers. The red ring of fire crept down a quarter inch, then faded to grey. With a soft pinch he felt the warmth, still alive, but hidden, burning deep inside. Then he turned it down and pressed it hard into his dinner plate.

"General Slocum.."

"Yessir?"

"I'll leave the Colonel in your care tonight."

"Yessir."

It was the first time Slocum had spoken. He looked over at his old friend. Alfred nodded back, hiding relief.

Sherman rose.

All followed.

"That will be all tonight, gentleman. We push them out tomorrow."

19

JIM FELL ASLEEP AFTER MIDNIGHT, legs out in front of him, back propped against the wooden railing. His arms were crossed over his chest, holding on to what was left of warmth. It was a deep sleep, and when he woke at sunrise to the steady beat of a brigade on the road, it took a minute to remember where he was. When he did, he felt it all again.

The prisoners were already on their feet, in line for breakfast. Jim got up stiff and quick and walked to the end. He was handed a tin plate with a hard biscuit, a slice of cold salt pork, and one steaming boiled potato. He ate it fast, all of it, while the other prisoners, most of them older, took their time. Then he held the empty plate in both of his hands, unsure what to do with it.

Ben saw his unease and walked over to him.

"I told you they'd feed us." He was smiling again. "Cheer up, son! The war's over for you."

"I just want to go home."

"Won't be long." Ben flicked the plate in Jim's hands with his middle finger. It made a loud "ping" and people looked and Jim was nervous.

"It'll be ok, man. Just do what they tell you."

A dozen bluecoats approached the pen in formation. The boys looked up. A Captain approached and opened the gate.

"Stack your plates in the center! We're moving to the rear!"

20

GENERAL SLOCUM WAS DRESSED AND READY before the sun. He had let Alfred sleep in his tent, and Alfred was spun up from dinner and stuck in a mire of embarrassment about being captured. Slocum had brought up old friends to change the subject. It had worked, but he still didn't get any sleep. In the glow of nostalgia, they talked all night about all that had been in Charleston: the women they both knew, the hunts, the hounds, the horse races. It was all in the past, but the old feeling of youth stirred them still. Sometimes the good ol' days are still good, and anything beats a war.

Slocum left Alfred lacing up his boots and went to see Sherman for instructions. The General was soaking up the morning, sipping a tin cup of coffee in a chair outside his tent.

"Give him back to Kil." Sherman said. "He'll knock him down a few pegs."

Slocum saluted and walked back to his tent. Alfred still hadn't finished dressing.

"Come on, man. It's time to go."

Alfred was silent. The courtesy had ended. The thought of months in a Yankee prison had begun. The man in grey and the man in blue left the tent and weaved through the village of canvas to the rear where the calvary was camped. Slocum pointed to a group of men.

"I'll have to leave you with General Kilpatrick. I've instructed him to treat you with the respect of an officer."

"Not that puppy again!"

"I don't have a choice, Alfred. My brigade's moving out today."

"I understand." Alfred accepted his fate, stiffened up, and gave a high-chined salute to his old friend.

"Until we meet again."

Slocum returned the gesture, and Alfred watched him until he was out of sight. Then he looked back slowly at the group of men in blue. The group saw him and quickly disbursed. Only Kilpatrick remained. He was waiting for him, and he was smiling.

21

THE BULL PEN AT THE TAIL OF THE BLUE SNAKE was made of fresh pine boards stacked six feet high. It was tight inside, a quarter acre of ground for a few hundred rebels, all fighting for space around a fire in the center. The sun was breaking through broken clouds, but it was windy on the backside of the rain and not yet warm. If you were a mourning dove that morning, jetting off your roost in the Black River swamp, you'd have looked down and seen the brown heads of two boys separated from the rest, propped shoulder to shoulder, facing the sunrise. Jim had never liked crowds, though Ben didn't seem to mind.

When the light cleared the top of the pines, the cannons began firing in the north, and the ground rumbled up through their numb feet and into their shins. The fight was back on, but all the boys could do was stand and watch the train of men and machine as it passed them toward the battle. Jim thought about the men around the campfire by the river, and he thought of Moore, and the sunken eyes of that man in the trees. They were all brave, or at least they seemed to be, but how could anyone face this much power?

The distant crack of a line of rifles made Jim flinch and the blue cannons answered the call. The earth was shaking hard now, and a stack of boards fell nearby, leaving a hole in the side of the pen. The men inside all turned and looked, but no one budged. Jim scanned the crowd and saw a group of rebels talking near the fire. They looked restless, but he couldn't hear what they were saying. Three blue soldiers began picking up the mess, sliding the boards back into place. Then the gate opened, and everyone stared.

A rebel officer walked in slowly and stepped toward the fire. The prisoners in the center parted, making room. The officer reached the fire and stood for a minute, warming his outstretched hands, eyes straight ahead, staring at nothing in plain disgust. Then he turned and walked to the corner. The men there scooted away too, and the officer stood there, alone.

The men in the center regrouped and leaned in toward one another, whispering something. Jim watched as one by one they looked up, then drew their heads back into conference. They were clearly upset. Jim looked back at the officer in the corner.

"I know that man."

"Of course you do." Ben was whispering. "Everyone does."

"What's his name?"

"That's Colonel Rhett, from Charleston."

A tingle hit Jim's spine and ran down into his arms.

Simmons.

Jim whispered as low as he could. "Didn't he kill a man in a duel?"

Ben's eyes sharpened on the colonel in the corner with a seriousness that was new to Jim.

"He killed a lot more than that."

"What do you mean?"

"Just watch..."

The boys sat still, trying to take in the scene without staring at the colonel who had taken a seat on the only pine log inside the pen. A shoeless man looking about thirty years old broke away from the conference and walked over to within ten feet of the colonel.

"What's he gonna do?" Jim was nervous.

Ben didn't answer. He just stared.

The shoeless man held up his right arm and pointed a dirty finger.

"Look at me you rich bastard."

The colonel looked away.

"I said look! You heard me the first time! You know what you did!"

Another rebel, about the same age, but blond and dirty, saw this and walked over and stood beside the shoeless man. He was pointing too.

"You and your god damn daddy are the reason we're in this hell. Look at you...with your pretty clothes and your fancy boots." The man turned to two Union guards who were watching the commotion from behind in the rail.

"Turn your backs, guards! We're gonna take him up out of those boots!"

The colonel showed no expression.

The blond man took two steps forward.

"I said look at me! I'll kill you before this war is over if it's the last thing I do!"

"Cool it!!! Or we'll shoot all a y'as!" The guard's sharp northeastern accent cut through the pen.

The two rebels smiled slyly in response, satisfied with their disturbance. They lowered their arms, stared at the colonel a little longer, then walked back to their conference in the center.

For the rest of the morning, the two boys in the pen waited for a fight that never came, while the guns of war echoed through their bodies. The colonel didn't flinch with the cannon-fire. He was somewhere else. Still as a statue. Blue eyes off in the distance. Searching for a world that used to be.

22

THE FIRING DIED OUT WITH THE DAY, and by evening the boys were tired and bored. They were handed biscuits through the rail for dinner, and they passed around a dozen metal canteens filled with water that tasted like rain. Jim ate the hard biscuit quickly and watched the colonel, still alone on his pine perch across the pen. The colonel took a bite of his biscuit, held it out in front of him, muttered something under his breath, and chucked it over the railing.

"Guess Colonel Rhett ain't used to this." Ben was watching the colonel too, and he was whispering.

"Why are they so upset at him?" Jim whispered back as low as he could.

"We was on our ways up here…" Ben leaned in close.

"That first one… without any shoes. He's from near Florence. He had a little brother about our age. We was camped a few miles from his momma's house. The little brother asks his Captain if he could go see his momma. Captain says no. We got too many deserters as is. Well the boy, I think his name was Christopher, he sneaks off and sleeps in his momma's house." Ben's brow wrinkled hard, and he shook his head.

"What happened?" Jim prodded.

Ben drew a deep breath and let it out slowly. "The boy made it back before sun-up, ready to go and everything. Didn't miss a beat. But Colonel Rhett found out about it."

"He shot him, too?"

"Made us all line up and watch."

Jim looked toward the corner, but it was empty. He scanned the pen. On the far side, he saw the colonel. His face was pushed into the slits of the gate, and he was talking to a guard.

"What's he doin' now?" Jim whispered.

"He's getting out. Prob'ly scared for his life."

The boys watched as the gate opened, the colonel walked out, and the gate closed behind him.

Jim let out a strange laugh. "Damn it all, Ben. He'd just leave us all in here?"

"In a heartbeat!"

"I guess I ain't surprised. I can't imagine shooting someone on my own side."

"I couldn't either until I saw it." Ben's eyes were up in the memory.

"You think that's why we're losing?"

"No, that ain't why." Ben lowered his head and stared straight at nothing and threw a pebble across the pen. It died in the dirt.

"But I'll tell you one thing, Jim. It ain't helping anyone but him."

23

March 19, 1865

THEY MARCHED TWO-BY-TWO AT GUNPOINT without speaking, blue guards on the sides and in the back, ten miles northeast through the pine woods, then out through the wide, open, cotton country of the coastal plain. Half of the homes they passed in the fields were burned to the ground, and smoke still rose from the brick foundations. The lucky ones sat still, as they always had, holding their breath until the big blue snake was out of sight. The beast doesn't discriminate in war. It takes what it wants, and dumb luck is better than none. Keep quiet, and maybe it'll move on past.

They entered Newton Grove that afternoon, looped around the circle in the center of town to the right and took the road to Goldsboro. The tiny houses in the town were deserted, but as Jim looked at the last, sad square in the row he saw the wide, white-eyes of a woman and her child, peering out from under a tan window curtain. Jim waved his hand and tried to smile, but the eyes drew back, and the curtain fell, and he felt sad and foolish.

They left the little town with the sun at their backs, marching into mile-wide, unplanted fields, black in the wet spots, yellow in the sun, and bright green where the spring weeds had taken. Goldsboro was a two day's march, and men were falling out by the dozen. The Yankees pulled them to their feet and ordered them on. Jim felt trapped by the tedious pace. He never walked that slow, and he was hoping they'd keep on through the night when the rumble of cannons, far to the north, caused the column to stop in its tracks. Everyone waited, and everyone listened.

Twenty miles away, bugles were playing, orders were being shouted, and thousands of men and boys were charging through fields and forest into the left wing of Sherman's Army.

They were outnumbered three to one, twenty-thousand men in grey against sixty in blue. But they fought, and Jim heard it, and he knew it was where he should be. He thought of the boys in Company G of the Junior Reserves: Stephen and Peter and Little Tim. He wanted his rifle back in his hands, and he felt like shooting something.

"Sure doesn't sound like it's over, Ben." The cannons were hot, on top of one another now.

"No sir. I think we're missing the big one." But Ben didn't sound disappointed.

"It's gotta be Bentonville. Damnit. I should be there."

The rumble grew like thunder.

"Feel that? They must have a hundred cannons!"

A blue soldier on horseback rode down the left side of the column, then circled around and rode up the right.

"Keep moving! Keep moving!"

Another officer rode up from the rear.

"You heard him! All of you! Or we'll shoot you in the back!"

Disgust filled Jim's gut and rose up his chest and there it tightened. He pointed at the smoke in the field to the right of the road. The house was almost gone, but the owners had made it out. In front of the dying flame was a pile of furniture, chairs and tables and dressers, another pile of clothes, a bunch of big barrels, and stack of flour sacks. A bull and three cows stood still in the yard, tied to an old grey fence.

A wagon and a dozen men in blue broke off from the column and headed toward the smoke. They shot the bull first, but it didn't fall. They fired again, and the boys winced with the death bellow of the big black beast. The cows fell quickly. The men loaded up the loot. When the piles were gone, they headed for the barn in the back.

"Clara." Jim didn't hear himself say it.

"Your wife? What about her?"

"Why do they have to take everything?"

"This is a war, Jim. They're trying to break us, and it won't stop until they do."

"Who decides when we're broken?"

Ben took a long sigh. "Men do, I guess. Men in charge."

Jim imagined a group of men in suits around a table writing down rules for others to follow. But it seemed too simple. Some of them, the ones in charge, did fight, and the few he had seen were on his side.

"You mean men like Colonel Rhett?"

"He's just one man, Jim."

"He's in charge ain't he?"

Ben shook his head left to right, walked a few steps, then stopped and nodded.

"Yes. He is. But a man can't help how he's brought up, no matter how lucky he is."

"You really think he learned all that?"

"Most of it. I tried to tell you, Jim." Ben raised his right arm and stuck a hitch-hikers thumb over his shoulder, pointed straight to the south.

"It's different down there."

24

"Men having both nerve and self-sacrificing Patriotism must lead the movement and shape its course, controlling and compelling their inferior contemporaries."

-Robert Barnwell Rhett, Sr.

ALFRED WAS TWO MILES AHEAD, walking under gunpoint with two other captured officers. He looked behind him and saw the big blue train stretched out for miles, as far as he could see, and he hated it, and everything it stood for. It didn't help that he was being treated like a miscreant. Late in the day, the hate blended with denial, and later, a dash of apathy. Without his customary power, the War was losing significance. He had begun to accept, and even hope, that it would all come to an end. Maybe Sherman was right? It was a question of numbers, and the arithmetic didn't add up. Then he heard the cannons through the pines in the north, and he stood up straight and ready, but he was a few inches shorter now, and he no longer felt like a colonel.

Kilpatrick had taken his Russian boots on the first day of the march. As a crowd of Yankees gathered to watch, Kil held the boots up high and presented the prize to a loyal inferior, a short, stumpy man from Ohio. When the fat man slid them on, the boots came all the way up to his ass. It was ridiculous, and the men had laughed when the stumpy man strutted and danced in a circle.

"Look at me! Look at my chivalry! I'm aristocratic now!"

Alfred had ignored the scene until another officer threw a pair of dirty brogans at his face. He dodged the first shoe, but the second spun in fast and the wooden heel hit his chin. He stayed calm, feeling the start of the swell, taking it like he felt he should, with pride.

"Try walking a mile in those."

Alfred had stood in silent defiance, avoiding eye contact, until the officers grew tired of the game and mounted their horses. He sat down in the dirt and slid on the broken shoes, stood up, and fell in with the march. He felt the worn ridges of the prior owner's toes with every step, and it twisted his stomach.

That was miles ago. The shoes now fit his feet. As he waited with the frozen column he thought about running. North toward the sound of the battle? South to home? But the guard beside him yelled to keep moving. Alfred let his head fall as he stepped back in line.

***

Twenty miles north, on the field at Bentonville, Burnett Rhett left his artillery unit, mounted his horse, and rode across the front until he reached his older brother's brigade. When he had the South Carolinians' attention, he yelled so all could hear:

"We have just received news that France has recognized the Confederacy! Our allies are sending a fleet of warships to open our ports! Fight with fury today, and you will have relief...and victory!"

The men raised their guns and let out a screeching rebel yell. Then they charged head-first across an open field, into the left wing of the great blue machine.

They drove it back, for a time. It was reinforced with fresh flesh and steel.

Repulsed, the South Carolinians charged again.

And again.

And again.

Seven times they charged.

For their honor.

For their country.

For a lie they couldn't help but believe.

PART III

25

March 23, 1865

Goldsboro, N.C.

JIM SLID HIS BACK against the pine rail of the pasture and watched the campfires come alive in the clear spring dawn. Behind him, the officers in their side pen hadn't budged, and today seemed a lot like yesterday, albeit a little warmer.

The two pens shared a common fence and not much else. The boys had looked through the rail for a sense of direction, or spirit, or advice, but the officers stayed in their canvas, hidden for most of the day, emerging only for meals in unbuttoned coats and dirty socks. Jim thought that they knew it was over. It sure seemed that way. They were all just waiting for the headline in the paper.

The people of Goldsboro sang them songs, brought them food, and knitted them clothing. The boys stayed in their uniforms, now stiff and black with soot from the pine fires they huddled around each night. They simply couldn't give them up.

A few men jumped the fence and ran off in the night. They were spotted quickly by one of the 100,000 Yankees camping around the town. No one saw them after that, and a rumor spread that they were being hanged outside of town, but Jim didn't let himself believe it. He had finally gotten some rest. The sense of dread had faded, and he wasn't going to spoil it. He played in a few ball games and lost his belt in his first try at poker. He thought a lot, sitting quietly on his own for hours. This annoyed Ben, who seemed to be enjoying himself as he hounded the latest news.

"Won't be more than a few weeks now, Jim."

"Do you think they'll kill the officers?" Jim looked back over his shoulder.

"They're shipping out tomorrow."

"Where to?"

"New Bern, last I heard. Then a ship to some prison up north."

Jim wondered why they'd go through all that trouble if Johnson was going to surrender, and Ben saw the confusion on his face.

"We're still holding a lot of theirs, Jim. They need em' for exchanges."

Jim turned and peered through a gap in the wood. He was counting the tents and the officers standing near them when his eyes landed on Colonel Rhett. Jim stopped counting and stared. The Colonel was walking through the camp with a wool blanket rolled tight under his left arm. With his right, he pulled back a canvas flap and disappeared behind it.

"Didn't reckon' we'd see him again."

Ben rolled his eyes and stayed silent. Jim kept at it.

"Be good to have a blanket though."

Ben's smile turned into a smirk. "Prob'ly had it shipped in from Persia or some shit like that."

"They let them do that?"

"Nah. Some girl made it for him. I keep telling you…all you gotta do is walk the fence line and look sad. When they come near you just talk to 'em nice. Tell em' how pretty they are and how bad the fightin's been. I got half a sweet cake doin' that yesterday. Everyone loves a hero, and these Goldsboro girls ain't different."

"A hero? We got captured, Ben. It ain't like we won anything."

"Yeah, maybe. But we didn't quit, and these people know that." Ben leaned back against the rail, locked his fingers behind his head, and stared up at the sky. His eyes landed on a red tail riding the drafts of the blue ether. "These people…they still got family off fightin'. They got friends that were killed."

"Can't everyone be a hero, Ben. Otherwise it don't mean shit."

Ben smiled at the sky. "You're too hard on people. That's your problem." Ben's gaze came back to earth and his head twitched to the right. "Don't stare, Jim. But see that boy across the way…"

Jim looked and saw a short boy sitting alone twenty yards down the fence line. He looked serious, like he was figuring out a math problem in his head.

"…He lost his daddy and both of his brothers in the same battle. Think about that a minute. He ain't a hero to you?"

"I guess he is. But no one's gonna know about it. Heroes get their names in books and newspapers."

"Not all of them do." Ben stood up quickly. "And if you're gonna ruin this pretty day, I'm gonna go get me another cake."

Jim laughed from below. "Go on then! Bring me some this time."

26

JIM STAYED IN THEIR SPOT for most of the afternoon, glancing every few minutes at the short boy that Ben had told him about. The boy was small and thick, with a big wide head and a cap too small for it, but he looked tough. The boy had moved half-way through the day, and now he sat alone against the rail shared with the adjacent pen that held the officers. Every ten minutes, like clockwork, the boy would turn and look behind him.

Jim was fascinated. But he made eye contact one too many times, and he saw the boy get up. Jim turned his head away quickly, but when he looked back up, the boy was glaring at him and closing fast. Jim stood up, half embarrassed, and reached out his right hand to greet him. The boy balled both of his fists and punch-pushed Jim's chest. Jim lost his balance, and a fence board cracked as it stopped his fall.

"What the hell you starin' for?"

Jim was having trouble breathing. He tried to apologize but gravelly air came out.

"Sorrrr…I…"

The boy looked disgusted. "Leave me alone, or it'll be worse next time."

Jim stood still, trying to find his breath but his lungs were closed tight. The boy turned and walked away, and Jim sat down with his knees out in front of him. He covered his face with his hands and couldn't resist watching the boy through his fingers. The boy walked back to the same place, then he turned and glared at Jim. Jim kept his face covered, and soon the boy was back to it, turning around, looking through the fence for someone or something.

Whatever it was, it seemed all the more important when mixed with violence, but Jim wasn't going to be caught twice. He turned his body away from the boy. Ben came back and slid down next to Jim with a shiny new grin on his face.

"How'd that feel?"

"Hurt like hell. What's he doin' over there?"

"I don't know, Jim. But I ain't gonna be the one to ask him."

27

ALFRED FINISHED HIS LETTER on the back page of Revelation 22. It was the only paper he had. The leaves were wavy and yellowed with age, and the back cover of the Bible was cracked in half. An old Presbyterian priest had handed it to him as they marched into Goldsboro. The priest looked defeated, sunken in his faded black robe, and Alfred had looked away, but the old man followed him and placed it against his chest. Alfred had nodded and thanked him and tried not to cry himself.

During the solemn, still afternoons, when there was still enough light in his tent, Alfred would thumb a random page and read the scripture. It was a slight reach for hope that never stuck. He'd never been religious, deciding in his teenage years to live in the real world. So a week later, when he found half of a broken pencil on the ground on his way to breakfast, he slid it slowly in his pocket and started forming a plan.

The sun was down now, behind the big pines, and the scheme took form with the night. Two yellow pages from the back of the Bible were crumpled in his jacket pocket. On these pages were letters, both to his father. He would throw them in the fire in the morning. The third, the one he stuck with, and the one still attached in the back of the Bible, was made out to:

A.B.R., Artillery, S.C.

In tight cursive, Alfred had written everything he knew about the size and scope of Sherman's force and the rumors he'd heard about where it was headed. He'd done this to save face, to look important, and to ensure it would be read by an officer, but all he cared about was the last sentence:

A.M.R. to New Bern, two day's time.

He hoped for a rescue, but he'd take an exchange. Blood matters above all things, and his little brother would help.

28

JIM KEPT HIS EYES OFF THE BOY until the pen fell into darkness. When he did look, he squinted, feigning sleep. The boy hadn't moved all day, and in the glow of the closest campfire, Jim could see the same angry look on his face. Jim put his hand under his coat and rubbed the bruise on his ribs. He didn't feel the sharp sting that comes with a break, and he figured he'd feel better in a few days, but damn, that kid could hit.

Ben was lost in dream, curled up on his side a few feet away. Jim nearly dozed off himself once or twice, but he watched the boy late into the night, his mind fighting off sleep until he had an answer.

It came after midnight. The boy rose and stood with his back to the fence. Jim sat up straight and squinted hard into

the darkness. The shadow of a tall man approached the fence behind the boy. The boy slid a book under his coat.
The shadow moved away, and the boy started down the fence line in some kind of hurry.

Jim knew better than to follow him.

29

ALFRED WANTED TO CRAWL INTO A REAL BED. The hard ground didn't suit him. But he was a field soldier now, and he believed that despite the terror of the past few years, his blood still carried enough fire to beat back the darkness. So he wrapped himself as best he could against the seeping east wind that never seemed to die in March, and he held onto his last remaining hope, penciled into The Good Book, and carried in the arms of a boy.

The kid seemed serious enough. A Patriot at heart, though a bit stupid. There was a decent chance he would make it. It was only twenty miles, and who looks out for a nobody?

He had promised the kid money and glory in return, and he would honor his promise after the war if it worked. If it didn't, add another name to the list. When what's left is no longer good, it isn't hard to gamble.

The alternative was shame, and Alfred already had his fill. Parts of him fell away with every step of compliance, and if the fire went out completely, he knew he'd never get it back.

30

SOMETHING HAD JIM BY THE SHOULDER. Then it hit his chest. He ducked away and pulled and twisted but he couldn't shake it off. He reached for his rifle and felt only air. Then he saw it, propped on the far bank of a rolling river.

"You gotta come see this!" Ben was shaking him hard.

"Ok. Ok." Jim wiped the sleep from his eyes and held up his arms and stretched the stiffness out of his back.

Ben was already walking away. "Come on man. Hurry!"

Jim looked around and saw that his side of the pen was empty. Most of the men had formed into a crowd in the far corner. Jim started walking and sped up and followed Ben's back through the bodies, bumping shoulders and apologizing quickly, in and out and around until Ben stopped. Jim came up next to him.

A half-dozen men in blue had the boy face-down on the ground.

"What's goin' on, Ben?" Jim whispered.

Ben didn't answer. He only stared ahead as they lashed the boy's arms behind his back and tied his feet together.

"You thought you could get by us!"

A soldier put his foot on the boy's back for leverage and heaved the knot tight. Then they pulled him back to his feet. He started to wobble, then he fell slowly, like a river tree, and Jim heard the thud as his head hit the earth. The blue soldiers laughed at this. Then they grabbed him and pulled him back up.

"Look at him. Thinks he's brave, but can't even stand up."

The boy stood red-faced in wobbly defiance against them, refusing to acknowledge the abuse. This only angered them more, and two took hold of him. The boy's shoes made two parallel lines in the dirt as they drug him up against the fence.

"Sit back down!"

The boy only looked straight ahead, so they pulled his feet out from under him and he fell again. This time he held his head up and his shoulder took the fall.

"He's a brave one, ain't he? Boy wants to be Robert E. Lee."

One of the blue soldiers took a half-burned stick from a cold campfire a few feet away. He tapped the boy on the head with the stick for show, then he stood over him and used the stick to write on the fence above the boy's head.

SPY

In big black letters.

"Colonel Rhett!" Jim didn't bother whispering.

Ben threw a sharp elbow in his rib.

"Shut up, Jim. Not now."

The soldier threw the stick on the ground and turned to face the crowd. He pointed at the boy beneath him.

"Take a long look at this traitor. We aim to hang him. And let it be a lesson to every one of you who still wants to fight."

The boy was wide-eyed and beet-red with rage, but he didn't speak, and he didn't move. The bluecoats walked toward the closest gate, and the crowd of prisoners began to file away. Jim and Ben stood still. The boy rolled on his side and pushed out with his legs and slid himself up against the fence. There he sat, propped under the letters, with the same stern defiance on his face.

Ben took Jim by the arm.

"Come on. We can't stay here."

31

BEN STAYED BY JIM'S SIDE THAT DAY. It was pretty in the field and warmed up good, but Jim was lower than the towhee that skipped the fence line, kicking up the wet dirt in search of spring bugs. Jim followed the little bird's lead, prying small pebbles from the ground until his fingernails hurt and flicking them for distance as he stared across the field to the corner. Ben caught him looking and threw a fresh warning.

"Does your wife know you have a death wish?"

"I saw him take something last night."

"Yeah...Well...He got caught."

"Colonel Rhett gave it to him."

"More reason to stay out of it!"

"B..." Another elbow from Ben stopped Jim's sentence.

Ben got up, put his hands on his hips, and stood over his friend.

"I ain't gonna let ya, Jim. It ain't worth it."

Jim rubbed the sore spot on his rib.

"I swear to God, Ben. If you hit me one more time…"

Ben opened his hands in welcome.

"What? What are you gonna do, Jim?"

Jim got up and pushed himself through Ben and began to walk away.

"Go on then. It's your funeral."

Ben waved a mock goodbye, but Jim didn't turn around. He began to pace the field around the fence line, slow and steady, trying to cool down and make sense of it all. When he got near the boy, he cut inside and kept his distance. He did the same when he got to Ben. Ben saw him and waved at him again and shook his head "no." Jim looked away and kept on walking.

He tried to imagine he was somewhere else. He couldn't. Then he thought about Clara and worried for her and wondered what she was doing. He'd heard the rumors, about it being over, and he pondered when he might see her again, but the pen was getting fuller by the day. He looked for new faces. They always sat alone, half scared and quiet, but they only looked new for a day or two. Then they formed into bunches and fell in with the rhythm.

Most of them at least. The boy was still there after Jim's twentieth lap, tipped over on his side with his shoulder back in the dirt. Jim got a little closer on his next pass, where he knew the boy could see him. He looked long at him, but the boy didn't budge. Jim finished the circle and sat back down beside Ben.

32

THERE WAS NO SUNSET THAT NIGHT. The thunderstorm was draped in grey, northeast to southwest across the fall line. It gathered strength as it slid down onto the coastal plain and tucked Goldsboro into bed with sheets of big, peppering rain and five minutes of hail in the worst of it. The fires were all put out in the wash, the moon was still unrisen, and the field was pitch dark and quiet. Jim rose wet and heavy and crept across the black, soft ground with purpose.

The boy in the corner was still lying on his side. His face and his uniform were covered with a layer of grey silt. As Jim leaned in closer, he saw the white slits of half-open eyes.

"I knew you'd be back."

Jim flinched and tried not to show it.

"Can I help you up?"

"Yeah. That'd be alright. Just pull me back a little."

Jim walked around behind the boy, bent down, and reached under his shoulders. In two big heaves the boy's back was against the fence. Jim crouched down and met the boy face to face.

"You got any food on ya? They ain't fed me all day."

"No. I wish I did."

"Oh. Well, that's alright. I don't need a last meal anyhow."

"Last meal?"

"They're taking me out tomorrow afternoon."

"Out to where?"

"Some kinda meeting with some judges…then probably a firing squad."

Jim imagined the boy blindfolded in front of the line and the rise of the smoke as the Spencers did the dirty work. He took a deep breath, then he said it.

"I saw you take something from Colonel Rhett."

"You did, eh?" The boy perked up. "I knew you was a sneaky shit!"

Jim didn't answer. The boy turned his head to the right and pointed with his eyes.

"Took off to the west. Almost got through, too. Made it a mile in the trees. There's just too many of 'em."

"I know." Jim stood up and looked behind the railing to see that they weren't being watched by the night guards that circled the fence like sheepdogs. The coast was clear, so he sat down next to the boy, shoulder to shoulder.

The boy felt the pouring out of someone who has been alone too long and finally has some real company. Jim saw a tear slide down his face.

"My daddy. Both my brothers. Now I guess it's me."

"Anything I can do for ya?"

"Just tell the Colonel what happened to me."

"I can do that. You want me to stay here tonight?"

"Nah. Don't want 'em to think you're part of it. They'll just suck you up too."

Jim looked over both of his shoulders, then rose to his feet.

"I'll do it. First chance I get."

Jim reached out his arm instinctively for a handshake, instantly remembered the boy's arms were tied, and felt embarrassed. He balled the hand into a fist and thumped the boy in the shoulder.

"I owe you one of these."

"Ha! I guess you do!" But the boy's smile faded fast.

"Don't worry. I'll talk to him."

"I'm not worried. You've got honest eyes. You'll do what you say."

"I'm gonna go. Keep your head up."

"Tell me your name first. You might be the last friend I ever have."

33

THE MORNING SUN ROSE SHARP through the top wiry needles of the pines, and the black shadows of the trunks looked like fallen monarchs on the ground, all toppled by the same force. Jim felt the light and the warmth on his cheek as he pinched his left eye closed and squinted through the thin gap in the boards with a bleary right.

He had been standing since sunrise, waiting for the Colonel, rehearsing ways to start a conversation that terrified him. None of them stuck. He had missed breakfast, Ben hadn't come back, and he was starting to lose hope. A half-dozen rebel officers had come out of their tents, and Jim wondered if the Colonel had already shipped out and what he would say to the boy, but he didn't give up. He would stand there all day if he had to.

It only took ten minutes. The Colonel emerged from his canvas in an unbuttoned jacket and pants that sat six inches above his dirty brogans. His face was unshaven, and his red hair was greasy against his head and slicked to the side. Jim kept staring. The Colonel didn't see him. Jim slid his hand through the gap and waved slow, then quicker, and the Colonel saw the outstretched arm and began to walk towards him.

As the Colonel got closer, Jim felt his hand start to shake. He pulled his arm back to his side, clenched his fist, and stood straight. He saw parts of the Colonel in pieces, but he couldn't quite put the man together. Jim took another step back, and the broken image seemed to grow. Then it started talking in a way that Jim had never heard before.

"Were you trying to gain my attention?"

Jim locked his shaky knees and clenched his fists tighter.

"Yessir. The boy who carried your book. They caught him. They're gonna shoot him today…unless we do something."

What would you have us do?"

"I thought…since you gave it to him…you could tell them that….and they're not gonna shoot an officer."

Jim heard a quick, dismissive sigh, and the man behind the fence got smaller. Jim stepped forward, put his eye in the gap, and saw the back of the Colonel as he walked away.

"Please sir! I promised him I'd talk to you."

Jim squinted harder. The Colonel disappeared behind the tents.

"Damnit. What do I do now?"

Jim stood there and waited, hoping that the Colonel would come back. He didn't. Jim slumped away slowly, back to his place. Ben was waiting for him. He met Jim half-way and leaned in quietly.

"What the hell are you doin' talkin' to Colonel Rhett?"

"I don't wanna talk about it, Ben. I know what you're gonna say."

"Well, you ain't gonna get any answers from him."

"Why is that?"

"Cause you ain't like him. And he feels like he ain't gotta give you any."

"They're gonna kill that boy, Ben. They're gonna shoot him."

"And you're gonna save him somehow?"

"I don't know, Ben, but I'm gonna *try*."

"Why?"

Jim reached down and picked up the closest rock. He slung it side-arm, and it smacked the fence like a mini-ball.

"I don't know, Ben. I guess there ain't much else to do anymore but try to save someone's life."

Ben sensed the shift in his friend, and he wasn't going to argue.

"You want me to help you?"

"Not yet. But thank you."

"Alright then. I'll get out your way."

Ben walked away. Jim took a few steps, sat down, and leaned back against the fence, trying to think of what else he could do. Then he turned and sat sideways, searching for the right words, and peering through the gap every few minutes for the chance to say them.

The chance never came. By noon, he heard the rattle of a wagon train and the whooshing flop of tents in the pen behind him. The brass was shipping out, and he didn't see the colonel.

He left his place and hurried down the fence line toward the corner, but before he got close, he could see that the boy was gone. All that was left were footprints in the dirt and three charcoal letters on the fence above them. Jim walked up to the fence and spit on the "S" and smeared the word into a black streak with the underside of his fist.

"Sons of bitches."

Jim jumped up and grabbed the top of the fence with both hands. He pulled hard until his chin reached the top. His eyes scanned the field beyond for the boy, but all he saw was blue. Jim let go and fell back to earth in defeat. Then he walked slowly back to his place.

He was twenty feet away when he saw the broken shadow of a man behind the fence. The shadow was waiting for him, but this time, he wasn't afraid.

34

THREE OFFICERS WERE SITTING AROUND a square wooden table, eating their lunches on white china they had borrowed from the cabinet of the three-bedroom house on Ash Street that was now their office. It had been a busy morning, and they were eager to wrap it up when two young soldiers appeared in the doorway. The officers pretended not to see them, but the two soldiers stood silent, waiting to be addressed.

"What is it now?"

"We caught a boy trying to escape. He was carrying something."

The soldier who spoke nudged the skinny, tall soldier next to him. The tall soldier walked toward the desk carrying an old Bible in his hand. He opened the book and placed it down in the center of the table, next to an open glass jar of molasses. The officers glanced down without expression and kept chewing.

The tall soldier stepped back and waited.

The middle officer looked at both of his comrades. They didn't budge. He didn't expect them to. He tilted up his glass and finished it. Then he wiped his face with the back of his hand and stood up.

"Fine. I'll see to it."

The officer walked slowly past the soldiers to the front door and looked outside. At the bottom of the steps, a young rebel was standing with his hands tied behind his back and his legs tied together. He couldn't have been more than sixteen. The officer let out a tired sigh and walked back to the kitchen.

"Bring him in there." The officer pointed across the hall.

"Yessir." The soldiers hurried out.

The parlor was a makeshift courtroom, with a big oak desk, three tall chairs behind it, and two smaller mismatched chairs in front. Two American flags stood at attention in the corners. The officers walked in and took their seats. The soldiers pushed the boy ahead and stood behind him.

"Untie him."

The soldiers took off the ropes. The boy kept his hands behind his back and didn't move his feet. His chin was high in the air.

The middle officer opened the Bible, scanned it quickly with crumpled brow, and looked up at the boy. Then he read it again, slower this time. When he finished, he slid the book to the officer to his left. The left officer read it fast with no expression, then slid it back to the middle. The middle officer slid the book to the officer on the right. The right officer read it, then read it again, his thick eyebrows rising in surprise.

Then he slammed it shut and slid it back to the middle.

"Have a seat young man."

The boy sat down and stared out the window.

The officer in the middle waved the two guards away.

"Wait outside, gentlemen. We'll handle this one."

35

JIM APPROACHED THE SHADOW SLOWLY, and he heard the same voice.

“Before they move us out, I would like an audience with you.”

Jim stepped in closer. A sharp blue eye hovered in a gap between the boards. He tried to see into it.

“I’m here, Colonel.”

“We have all made sacrifices in this great conflict. Some more than others. But we are fighting for all that makes life enjoyable.”

“No one can stop Sherman, Colonel. The war’s over and everyone knows it!”

“As long as I’m standing, the war’s not over!” The voice was hot and high. “Liberty is not a reward for the weak!

It took seven years to defeat the British. We've only been at this for four. We go on to the end, or until they kill all of us!"

"But they took the boy! He's gone!"

"Speak no more of it! And remember who you fight for. He did."

Jim turned away from the shadow, but it called out to him from behind.

"That boy gave his life for the Cause! There can be no higher honor!"

At ten paces, Jim turned.

"No he didn't, Colonel. He gave his life for you."

PART IV

36

THREE OFFICERS WERE STARING AT A BOY. The boy's head was turned, and this annoyed them immensely. His young eyes were fixed on the manilla wall. The wall was old and faded, except for a square half-way up, about two-feet wide, where a portrait used to hang, blocking the paint behind it from the afternoon sun.

"Look at us boy."

The boy didn't.

"What are you staring at?"

The boy turned to face them.

"I was thinking about the family that used to live in this house before you stole it."

The officer in the middle coughed in disgust. He looked at the others. They kept staring at the boy. Then he opened the Bible and held it up in his hand.

"The author of these words is guilty of treason. We know a rebel officer wrote it."

The boy didn't flinch.

"Listen, son. I've seen too many your age dead along the way. I don't believe another execution will serve our cause. But you're going to have to tell the truth if you want any clemency from your government."

"What truth do you want? You seem to have it figured already."

"We need to hear it from your lips. We know the character of your leaders. We know what men like them can do to people. But we all make choices. You made a choice, and you may lose your life for it."

"I knew that when I signed up."

"There's nothing left to fight for boy! Richmond's lost. Johnson's trapped. This nightmare's coming to an end. I imagine you'd want to spend the rest of your days in peace."

A deep flame rose inside the boy and his face flushed with fire as he stared at the Yankee across the desk.

"I won't ever have peace."

The officer looked to his left and his right, and the three men nodded. .

"So be it."

37

ALFRED WAS PULLING HARD AS HE ROWED. He was close now, almost to the Southern Wharf that stuck out from the safety of the city into the sweep of the Cooper River. A crowd of fancy people stood along the dock, and they were cheering. His father stood apart at the end, smiling, and waving him in.

Alfred lifted his hand to wave back and felt a shock of ice in his toes. When he looked down, cold water swirled around his feet, and the white wood of the deck was gone, replaced with yellow parchment. He rowed with all his might and looked for something that would float, but the paper skiff was empty. On the port side he saw the signatures of two dozen men. On the starboard was a date:

July 4, 1776

The harder he pulled the worse it got, and the water in the boat turned black. It stained his ankles and rose up his shins, and he threw away the oars.

When he awoke, he was still in North Carolina.

The End

Author's Note

I have wrestled with the South my entire life. It's beautiful and awful, but it's real. Alfred Rhett was a real man. He was captured a few miles from my hometown. He shot his own soldiers, and he bragged about it at dinner with Sherman. I tried to understand why. The answer was a work of fiction.

Jim McClaren is a product of my imagination. Give him a fitting end in yours.

The poems that follow were written early on, when I tried to find the mood to write this story.

In the last analysis, we all get caught up in waves, and we're never the same after. I hope you enjoyed this one. I put my heart into it.

-Matt Richardson

POEMS FROM THE BEGINNING

Memory / Boys in Blue

Look up.
Feel that?

Warm, bright, not a cloud in sight.
The sun draws last night's rain from the sandbox of youth;
It rises in dizzy waves into a blue Carolina sky.
Loblollies sway in a stiff spring breeze,
And a circling red-tail claims his section of heaven.

Now take a breath.
It's nice, isn't it? Memory?

The yard. The spring. Bells. Birds. Bees.
Your father smiling on Sunday afternoon.
Hasty azaleas burst in pink and white;
Didn't your mother plant those?

Do you remember her?
Broad, bright and five-feet high;
Commanding your attention.
You should try.
Petals fall with the next big rain.

"Look away," she tells you,
"It's all just a dream."
And heed her advice.
Once you see us, you can't forget.

But you looked anyways. You always did.
How does it feel being never the same?
Welcome to the new world.
What's done is done.
Besides, flowers have no memories.
Not yours, anyway.

Yours are black and charred to the stem;
Lit up like Moses by us boys in blue.
And your big white house?
We'll take that too.

"Look away," she told you.
But you didn't learn,
How to move on with time,
Now your memories burn.

The Grind

Hitch them up to that caisson; it's bogged down again.
Pull, and heave, and hammer.
Clean and reload.
The blue machine runs on blood, sweat, and grease.
Fed by rivers of steel, never stopping to sleep.
If it does, it dies, and all of us with it. So keep moving.

The machine gives us cash, clothes, guns, and glory.
It's all in the manual, so form up again.
That or go back to Brooklyn, where small machines whiz in
forgotten alleys.
You're an American, son, just like all the rest.
But our machine respects grind, not birthright.
If you're working hard enough. Are you?

Matter and energy cannot be created or destroyed.
God gave you yours to give to the machine.
Shouting the battle cry of freedom.
Down with the traitors, up with the stars.
Not a man shall be a slave.
As long as the big machine keeps turning.

Look up ahead, more idiots in the road.
They give more than the blacks in bondage.
Limbs, lives, sons, homes, and peace.
They've lost, and they all know it.
But the machine won't stop for them.
They work for other masters.

One Guarantee

Evil birds on the wing,
Float on winds of destruction.

In a guise of equality, blue feathers spread;
And poison rains on Southern heads.

Cover the Great Contract in glass.
Its words will last if you let it.

It's there in black and white, solid as a headstone;
Plain, unfettered by the winds of change, cold.

Say what you want about it.
It gives you that right.

But paper and ink can't live and breathe,
When those that signed it are dead.

We inherited but one guarantee;
And we wished to keep it.

A Republic, for which we stand;
You have forgotten.

Lads and Lances

Boys flip the curtain of a forbidden sill,
Prodded by legend and youthful will.

A hermit sits in ages past,
For all that was and could not last.

The fire prod has turned to rust,
But in his hand, a mighty thrust!

Sparks of old rise in the night,
For love once lost in armor bright.

"It's him, I told you! Now you see!"
Curtain closes, two lads flee.

In wood nearby they claim their breath,
And with sapling spar to feign of death.

Lances fresh and bark shields high!
"Consider what it means to die!"

And if you don't, an unpaid cost:
The time to dwell in all that's lost.

POEM AT THE END

Whirlpool

Out of the empty,
The island appears again.
White sand under midnight sky.

You were there once;
Though you only remember the feeling.

And you only remember the feeling,
As you circle around and start again.
Drawn to something you never knew you lost.

www.ingramcontent.com/pod-product-compliance
Lightning Source LLC
LaVergne TN
LVHW090520110826
845146LV00003B/928

* 9 7 9 8 2 3 4 0 8 4 1 4 9 *